Netanya

Other Works in Dalkey Archive Press's Hebrew Literature Series

Heatwave and Crazy Birds
Gabriela Avigur-Rotem

Kin
Dror Burstein

Dolly City
Orly Castel-Bloom

Lily la Tigresse
Alona Kimhi

Homesick
Eshkol Nevo

Life on Sandpaper
Yoram Kaniuk

Motti
Asaf Schurr

Netanya

Dror Burstein

Translated by
Todd Hasak-Lowy

Series Editor
Rachel S. Harris

DALKEY ARCHIVE PRESS
CHAMPAIGN / LONDON / DUBLIN

Originally published in Hebrew by Keter Books, Jerusalem, 2010

First edition, 2013

Library of Congress Cataloging-in-Publication Data

Burshtain, Deror.
[Netanyah. English]
Netanya / Dror Burstein ; Translated by Todd Hasak-Lowy. -- First Edition.
pages cm
"Originally published in Hebrew by Keter Books, Jerusalem, 2010."
ISBN 978-1-56478-923-5 (alk. paper)
1. Burshtain, Deror. 2. Netanyah (Israel)--Biography. I. Hasak-Lowy, Todd, 1969-
translator. II. Title.
PJ5055.17.U7Z4613 2010
892.4'8703--dc23
2013033401

Partially funded by a grant from the Illinois Arts Council, a state agency

The Hebrew Literature Series is published in collaboration with the Institute for the Translation of Hebrew Literature and sponsored by the Office of Cultural Affairs, Consulate General of Israel, in New York.

Cover: design and composition by Tim Peters

www.dalkeyarchive.com

Printed on permanent/durable acid-free paper

Even when I say sun and moon and star
I mean things that happen to me
—Alejandra Pizarnik

In the summer of 2009, I read, with an amazement that turned, on occasion, into awe, Peter Ward and Donald Brownlee's book, *Rare Earth*; and it was at dusk, while reading their chapter on the moon, that I left my house, book in hand, lay down on the bench on my street in Tel Aviv—Smuts Boulevard—and stared up at the moon of the end of the month of Tammuz, unable to read any further. I now saw the moon as the authors of *Rare Earth* had taught me, not as the circle of light beloved of poets, and not as a sort of feeble oil lamp accidentally left burning above a city that no longer needs it, but rather as an essential factor, one among the myriad factors essential for the existence of life, and therefore my life as well, on Earth. I gazed at the moon and thought about what I'd just read, according to which the moon gives life to Earth in general and to me in particular thanks to three gifts, namely: the ebb and flow of the tides, the slowing down of the Earth's rotation in relation to the sun, and the stabilization of the Earth's axial tilt in relation to the sun at an angle enabling the existence of the seasons. So, with *Rare Earth* under my head and a bookmark stuck between pages 234 and 235, I decided to write these things down, and some time after that night of lying on the bench on my street I did indeed start writing them down in a notebook, and I continued with this for a month and a half, each and every day, sitting on the small wooden stool our guinea pig gnaws on and hides under. Among the various thoughts that flooded over me on the bench on Smuts Boulevard during the last days of July 2009 was a stubborn notion about Hebrew literature, in which I have resided all these long years like a tenant in a side room of a run-down old hotel catering to whomever can scrape together the price of a room. On that hard bench I realized that in all of Hebrew literature there isn't so much as a single mention of the astonishing fact that the movement of the continents, what we today call plate tectonics, and the formation of the moon are apparently the result of the very same event: an enormous body struck earth and created an ocean of magma—which eventually made plate tectonics possible—and sent a mass of rock flying into space, chunks that eventually seized hold of one another and spun until they made up a big ball and became the moon. And without plate tectonics, according to Ward and Brownlee, we wouldn't be alive today. But even this fact, the essentiality of plate tectonics, which regulates the temperature on Earth, Hebrew literature has kept hidden, like a stinky sock. Authors stare up at the moon or down at the Earth and write about kibbutz folk settling the land, with accordions and hoes and, of course, firearms in their hands. In Hebrew literature, land is always either solid ground or property, fenced off and registered with the proper office, it's not rock liquefying at a temperature close to that on the surface of the sun. Which is all well and good, yet no one writes about plate tectonics, or the Cambrian period, or trilobites. How strange, I said to myself as I lay on the bench, that in Hebrew literature, and this includes the literature of the Hebrew Enlightenment, there isn't even a single trilobite. What am I talking about, you couldn't even find a saber-toothed tiger or a dinosaur or a mammoth in Hebrew literature, not even in the great works of Brenner or Gnessin, and not because they didn't know of their existence, either. Indeed, Brenner, as is well known, worked for a time doing manual labor before World War I at the excavation site of a Russian delegation of fossil scholars in the Negev, and was among those who unearthed a wall of ammonites—those same beautiful, spiral-shelled creatures that became extinct along with the dinosaurs sixty-five million years ago, at the end of the Cretaceous period, and today bake in the desert sun at the Ramon Crater. For his part, Gnessin kept the fossil of a small flying creature on his writing desk, which a scholar of Hebrew literature has yet to identify, and this same fossil wandered with him from city to city and from writing desk to writing desk, through Kiev, Hommel, London, Petach Tikvah, and Pochep, until it finally came to rest on the table next to his bed in the Infant Jesus hospital in Warsaw, where Gnessin died of heart disease in 1913 at only thirty-four years of age.

It was shocking, I thought, that you go through all those years of school, and no one ever tells you to look upward at nighttime. No one. A few days before that long night during which I lay on the bench on Smuts, a giant comet crashed into Jupiter. Jupiter, because of its massive size and tremendous gravitational field, serves as a kind of breakwater for comets and asteroids, some of which, were it not for this, would hit Earth, causing the extinction of all or a large part of the life inhabiting it, as it appears indeed happened sixty-five million years ago. But sometimes Jupiter's gravitational field actually diverts objects and sends them toward us. You are watched over from a great distance by a guard who doesn't realize that he's been assigned to this task. He gets up in the morning and goes to his office in order to protect you and you yourself don't know it either. But sometimes his job changes, and suddenly he's your bitter enemy. I closed my eyes, raised my hands, and felt Jupiter's gravity pull at my fingernails and lengthen them. Rocks we don't see float above the sky, above the clouds, and Jupiter, that glowing point in the firmament, which most people, including most poets and writers, don't really look at and don't give much thought to, grants us life from day to day. If it weren't for Jupiter there'd be no pens and so that would be the end of literature,

I said to my neighbor, a well-known lawyer who once got me out of jail, and who while I was thinking all of this happened to pass by the bench with his tiny dog Cleopatra, but he continued walking down the sloping boulevard, seemingly led by the dog, who was drawn by the smell of cats, which were drawn by the smell of the dry food I scatter for them along the boulevard from a hundred-kilogram sack that I purchase and haul home on my back, sweating and panting, each week. But of course Jupiter is only one example among many: How flimsy our existence is, how many conditions *must exist and must continue to exist over the course of millions of years* so that a single flower or a single pencil or a single book might exist—this thought unnerved me that night on the bench and it unnerves me still. For a moment I felt like a string being strummed by thousands of fingers, and I closed my eyes. Our existence on this planet hangs by a thread, every tomato and every onion is such an enormous miracle you could collapse with awe in a vegetable market. So I lay there on the boulevard's bench. The street emptied out, television sets glowed from the houses. My neighbor and his dog receded down the boulevard's slope until they looked like two tiny points on the horizon. Had they turned toward me, had they come and lay down next to me on the narrow bench, I would have told them how at the age of fourteen, in Netanya, I studied astronomy and built a telescope. But the horizon had already swallowed them up and submerged them in its clouds. All the parking spots along the boulevard were taken. Night fell on the benches and on me.

. . .

It was in an astronomy class that took place at Remez House, the Workers' Council building on Remez Street in Netanya, which in the meantime has been destroyed. In 1984, I sat each week with a not very large group of kids and teenagers and learned about the

האם יש חיים בכוכבים אחרים???

לפי ההגיון יש חיים בכוכבים אחרים
כי יש מיליארדי כוכבים (שמשות) ולכל כוכב
כמעט יש כמה כוכבי לכת אז
לא יכול להיות שמתוך מאות מיליארדי
כוכבים רק בכוכב אחד והארץ
קיימים חיים. על מאדים לא יתכנו חיים
כי אחוז החמצן שם הוא כ- 3%. על
שבתאי לא יתכנו חיים כי יש שם
כוח משיכה עצום וגם מפאת ריחוקו
מהשמש שורר שם קור עצום. על
המאדים כמות המכתשים קטנה מזאת
שבירח. כי למאדים יש קצת אטמוספירה
וחלק מהמטאוריטים מתחככים באטמוספרה
ולא מגיעים
למאדים

משמאל: מערכת השמש

מימין: פני המאדים

(Translation: Is There Life On Other Planets??? According to reason there is life on other planets because there are billions of stars (suns) and for almost every star there are a few planets so it can't be that from out of the hundreds of billions of planets only on one planet, the Earth, life exists. On Mars there can't be life because the percentage of oxygen there is around 3%. On Saturn there can't be life because there is tremendous gravitational pull there and also due to its distance from the sun tremendous cold exists there. On Mars the amount of craters is smaller than that on the moon. Because Mars has some atmosphere and some of the meteors rub against the atmosphere and don't reach Mars. On the left: the solar system. On the right: the surface of Mars.)

solar system and nebulae and galaxies and Apollo 11. In my class notebook, which I have kept with me to this day, under the heading "Facts and Details," written in my childhood handwriting, which has barely changed since, are the following items:

"Every second the weight of the sun decreases by 4,000,000 tons because the weight of the sun is burning. To us 4,000,000 tons seems like a lot but to the sun that's nothing. If we took a grain of sand and gave it to a bug it would be very heavy for him but for us a grain of sand is very light. Therefore if you ask is a grain of sand light or heavy you have to answer in relation to us or bugs or someone else big or small. In about 13,000,000,000 [years] the sun will stop burning. The gas will run out and it will stop burning."

These things I am now writing, in the summer of 2009, are nothing more than an extension of my old astronomy notebook from the class in 1984. You write a few lines at the age of fourteen and near the age of forty you complete what you began a quarter century earlier. An old notebook goes with you from house to house until one day you open it and fill up the empty pages. You leave empty pages at the end of every notebook and at some point you have to fill them up. If you don't fill up the empty pages someone else will, and maybe he'll do it better than you. Every book is begun on a blank page at the end of another book, sometimes a book you wrote and sometimes a book by someone else. This is literature's great secret. The telescope I built then was a Newtonian telescope ten centimeters in diameter, whose concave lens I ground myself, with a lot of effort and with the help of powders and the guidance of my first astronomy teacher. Once a week I would go to his house and polish a round lens with different powders: at first you polish with coarse ones, and very slowly you replace them with finer ones. Eventually a concave lens is obtained, which you then coat in mercury. After this period of daily grinding and polishing I went up to the roof of our house on Bialik Street with my father and grandfather and pointed the telescope at the moon. At first I couldn't make anything out, until suddenly, after a few adjustments, the light of the moon filled the tube. I stood on a small stool and saw the craters. My grandfather sat by the edge of the roof, near the railing, and smoked. He looked up at the clouds as if none of this mattered to him, squashing his cigarette butts on the railing. "You don't want to see, too, Dad?" my father asked him, but my grandfather didn't answer. The two of us continued looking. The August wind of 1984 came from the sea nearby, and it seemed as if it was winter in Netanya. We explored the stars, but the telescope was too small to give us a good look at them, so we went back to scouring the sky with our bare eyes. We stood there with necks stretched back, and the light of thousands of stars, seen and unseen, trickled into our eyes. My eyes, which were born of the eyes of my father and the eyes of my mother, as all eyes are born, saw the stars that he saw. From eye to eye. From four eyes two eyes are born, not eight eyes as you might think. When a cloud covered up the moon, my father lowered the telescope toward his father (my grandfather) and signaled for me to be quiet. His father's (my grandfather's) face appeared upside down in the concave mirror, his knees and feet pointing up at the sky, and the smoke from his cigarette curling down. The telescope turns everything upside down. Man and star. I looked at my father looking at him. For some reason he continued to look at him as if he had discovered a new crater on the moon. My grandfather was nearby, perhaps six or seven meters away. We waited for him to realize we were looking at him and turn to face us, but he didn't notice a thing. The roof of the building served as an ashtray for him, and he put out cigarettes along its edge. My father raised his hand and waved to him, the way you wave to someone who comes into view at a distance, from the end of a street or on a boat's deck in the middle of the sea. But my grandfather didn't pay us any attention and kept on staring at the treetops.

The telescope I built at the age of fourteen caused me to lift my head and my eyes. For better or for worse—who knows. At the age of fourteen I had a subscription to *All the Stars of Light*, the journal of the Israeli Astronomical Association, and understood almost nothing of what I read. The pictures were black and white and quite blurry. In those days I would go up to the roof of our building on Bialik Street in Netanya and read issues of the magazine until sunset, my back to the sea and the waning light. The pages were washed in yellow and purple. The sun, in its final moments, struck the stars and clusters of stars on the pages and sometimes struck its own likeness there too, very small, gray, smaller even than my hand, which held it. In one of these issues there was an ad for an astronomy conference at Ben-Gurion University, and so, at the age of fourteen, I found myself sitting next to my father in a giant hall in the middle of the desert. I understood nothing of what was said, due to the fact that this astronomical conference actually dealt more with mathematics. In the adjacent hall, a conference was being held by the Department of Hebrew Literature, but this we didn't enter. The academics transformed the stars and the nebulae and white dwarfs into formulas and equations, that is, into mathematics, but I didn't succeed in understanding the connection between the numbers and symbols that filled their blackboard and the stars themselves. A young and apparently nervous researcher calculated the diameter of a black hole on the board, and one of the professors went up angrily to the lectern, knocked over a potted anemone plant, and ran a damp sponge over his calculations. From the adjacent hall, belonging to the literary people, faint applause could be heard. I dragged my father from the hall and we got into our car. At the top of a nearby hill a large camel chewed the air. We hoped to get on the main road heading north, but due to a navigational error (I had the map), instead of Netanya we arrived at the Ramon Crater. My father stopped the car by the side of the road, above the "Wall of Ammonites," which I know about today because the author Y. H. Brenner, who was a relief worker at the Russian delegation's dig, helped uncover it, a massive layer of large shells from the Mesozoic era, which seemed to appear suddenly before his eyes, as he writes, in the heart of the Negev on the side of the crater. Only then did my father understand our mistake. He pulled on the hand brake, suddenly, as if alarmed, and turned off the engine. Complete silence prevailed at the edge of the crater. We sat in the car for a few minutes opposite that massive pit and breathed. Afterward, we got out of the car. Fossils were stacked at our feet like a pile of white rugs. I was already quite heavy at that age, but nevertheless my father picked me up so I could see better—that over there, not far, a flock of ten or twenty sparrows hovered in the air at our feet.

. . .

The memories swarm on the other side of the tent's fabric, leaning in with their backs from the outside, like polar bears, weighing down the canvas. One word is enough, one star is enough to remind you of an old notebook, and already you're lost. Already you're on a blank page, and already you're stuck in Netanya, and already you're grinding a telescope mirror, and already you're not in what is called the present. I've been attacked by memories, I thought. They surround me like an asteroid belt, and from time to time one of them breaks away from its position and seeks out a new gravitational field. One day you're trying to recall the color of your grandmother's mother's eyes, and you don't even succeed in remembering her name; but on another day you're lying on a bench on a boulevard and all at once you sprout a beard of memories. In a bit you'll go up to your apartment and shave, yes. There you'll find the sharpened razor and fragrant foam of the present. Yes, in a bit, a towel will be spread out, there will be a great shave, and the smooth skin of your face, the true skin, will break through, will be revealed from beneath that unruly hair. But in the meantime you're far from home, the razor is so far away, and the fragrant, burning liquid you'll undoubtedly splash on your face years from now is still imprisoned in some distant land, in the bulbs of flowers waiting for the sun to rise and call out to them, *open*.

. . .

My classmates played soccer in the courtyard of Remez House, while I sat in a lecture hall and wrote down data about the solar system and quasars and neutron stars and pulsars and "white dwarfs." The astronomy teacher explained that the words "light year" do not indicate time but rather distance. When you stare off into the sky you're gazing into the distant past, he said. When he said "the distant past," a loud noise sounded above his head. A ball kicked from the courtyard shattered a window in the astronomy hall. The teacher clapped his hands. There you have it. The big bang. A small, thin pane of glass broke according to its own internal logic, a window that was at first utterly transparent and then all at once visible, all at once you hear the noise, and within a second everything is fixed, the entire future. Everything is contained inside that glass, he said. Indeed, there is no glass, he shouted, meaning there is only glass, it's all glass, and this transparency shattered. This is the transparency that shatters. Perhaps I should say shattered transparency. We were children and wrote down every word in our notebooks.

When Elan, one of my friends from class, entered the hall (which during the High Holidays served as a temporary synagogue where my grandfather, Zvi Burstein, was one of the cantors) breathing heavily, the astronomy teacher was pushing around shards of glass on the floor with a broom handle and naming them after star clusters and galaxies. With the toe of his sandal he had kicked the ball into a corner, where it sat for a few moments until Elan entered to return it to the soccer coach who was waiting in the courtyard. I kept my head down in my notebook, but Elan recognized me and gave me a look full of disgust. He took the ball and went back to the courtyard, and after a minute or two had passed the ball which was again kicked into the hall, intentionally this time, no doubt, shattering another window. The astronomy teacher bounced the ball on his knee a couple times and then kicked it back through the newly shattered window. He stood a moment in silence, looking toward the now vanished ball. Silence fell in the courtyard as well. Perhaps the game had ended or perhaps the rain that had started to fall drove the players away. One of the retirees who participated in the class announced, Cloudburst. Our class was also about to end, only the teacher didn't look at the clock. From his place next to the window he said that he now understood that it was possible the big bang hadn't been a unique and singular event and that there's no reason to think that whatever happened once, for no apparent reason—in other words the creation of the world—couldn't happen again in some distant corner of the universe; or, he added, and closed the almanac for the year 1984, in another universe, a parallel universe, and after a moment of silence pointed at the window, through which the sounds of the game could no longer be heard, and said: right here, right under our nose. Here is the distant corner. Perhaps it happened just now and we didn't notice at all. That same tiny nucleus in which everything was packed, visible matter and dark matter both, he said, still holding the broom, who knows if it isn't in the next room or even right here. I was fourteen years old. What could I have said? He was looking at the closet that was open and empty then but during the High Holidays served as the Holy Ark of the synagogue of the Workers' Council, in which my grandfather, as I have pointed out, was cantor. Then, of course, I didn't understand what "parallel universe" and "dark matter" meant, and I was more concerned with the matter of the ball and my fear that another window might shatter and hit my head, but the teacher wanted to end the lesson, and so, with a distant look, turned the broom right side up and swept all the broken galaxies of two universes into one pile. I leaned down and held the dustpan for him, and I remember the rattle of the broken glass being swept in and then the sound of glass shards sliding into the garbage can, which was the same exact garbage can that served the Remez House synagogue during the High Holidays and that stood right next to the podium against which my grandfather would support himself when passing before the Ark.

While I was lying on the bench on Smuts I recalled those four wondrous words: *passing before the Ark*. Out of them rose as well that frightening word *shofar*—the ram's horn blown to herald the New Year—and the words I most associate with the High Holiday prayer book, *The King*, which my grandfather would pronounce in the tones of a man pleading for his life. The words in the prayer book were printed in very large, thick lettering, and I remember kissing them, as a child, as though inside them, inside the printed letters themselves, lay a terrible secret. The words *The King* would also come back to me during my astronomy lessons, in those days; it rang in my head both then and during the High Holiday services that were held in the very same hall in Remez House, where my grandfather was cantor on Rosh Hashanah and Yom Kippur, and once, when I was four, prayed barefoot. My grandfather was the one who first took me to the observatory in Givatayim. This was before I built my own small telescope.

He himself, so he said to me, wasn't interested in looking at the moon through the large telescope at the observatory. The size of the telescope intimidated him. He was afraid, or so he confessed to me on our ride home, that he wouldn't be able to stand the sight of the moon and its powerful light at such magnification. And indeed, after I gazed for a few moments at the face of the moon through the telescope in Givatayim, I was dumbstruck and couldn't make a sound. I was flooded with light. The sight was more than I could bear after years of looking at pictures of the moon in black and white. It was too dazzling. Too sharp. Too close. Too real. I felt as though I were hovering above the surface of the moon at a low altitude and that I would fall into a round crater at any moment. I knew that if I only extended my leg I would be pulled down to the glowing white sands and the lunar shadows. I traveled to the moon via Givatayim's telescope, and crawled over its surface. I traveled to the moon. I curled up at the edge of the Mare Tranquillitatis, in the distance I saw the Apollo 11 lunar module, which was launched the year my mother carried me in her womb. I was looking forward to the morning. I hadn't brought a blanket with me to the moon. It occurred to me to crawl toward the lunar module and sleep inside it. Certainly I'd find food and a blanket inside, I thought, and I started crawling in its direction. A few moments later I saw the Earth rise over the horizon. I recognized the east coast of Africa, and I yelled so that they'd rescue me, the way we'd yell and wave from a desert island at the ships passing by, after our own boat had capsized.

From that evening until the next, I didn't speak to anyone. I didn't go to school or to astronomy class, and I barely ate. I lay in bed for a whole day and then another. I thought I was done with the sky once and for all. No one understood what had happened to me. On the third day, my astronomy teacher appeared at our home. Only years later was it brought to my attention that my teacher had, earlier that day, gone to the Um Khalid medical center in Netanya because of a nasty eye infection, and my grandfather, who worked as a clerk there, told him what happened and invited him to celebrate his birthday with us. My teacher wasn't at all surprised when he saw me. On the contrary, he said, both Galileo and Kepler tell of a similar effect after gazing at the moon "up close" for the first time. Its light flows into the open eye as if from a drainpipe. The moon has power, he said. Looking at it is like looking at the sun, for the moon reflects its light. They've invented sunglasses, he said sadly, but moonglasses—not yet. There's only one remedy for moonstroke, he said: building a telescope. And like a magician he pulled a clear round piece of glass from behind his neck and held it between finger and thumb under the light. I sat up in bed. Birthday cake floated through the air from the kitchen. On the frosting, in marzipan, as she did every year, my mother drew an immigrant ship in a calm sea, being chased by a furious Poseidon under a rising sun in the middle of the night in a bittersweet-chocolate sky.

In fountain pen on my grandfather's immigration form, the government of Palestine's immigration document number 48452, it is written that he left Warsaw on August 14, 1934, and two days later boarded a ship. Profession: laborer. Age: 19 1/2. Name: Burstein, Hirsch. Labor Federation membership: Israel Pioneer Association. Citizenship: Polish. Address abroad: Ciechanów. Arrived in the Land of Israel: August 26, 1934. Four days after this, on August 30, 1934, he left the Immigrant House. Knowledge of Hebrew: yes. All of this was recorded in the registry ten years before my father was born. And what I'm writing now, and my existence itself, were already folded away between the lines of that form. In fact, the book you are reading right now was begun by the clerk who recorded my grandfather's data onto that immigration form. Your grandfather's immigration form is the preface to your birth certificate, I said aloud to the air above the bench I lay on that night. How hard it is to see the future. If an immigration form can transform into a birth certificate, what does a birth certificate turn into? His pen is my pen, and with a rusty safety pin I can attach the immigration form to the notebook in which I write these lines, and then attach it to one of the copies of this book. I adjusted my position on the bench and ignored the looks of neighbors wandering around the boulevard like nighttime beachcombers. My eyes were fixed on a cloud above my head. In Svensmark and Calder's book *The Chilling Stars*, it says that the clouds above our heads are created thanks to cosmic rays emitted millions of years ago by suns that have exploded and whose lights have already gone out. Our sun's solar winds protect us from most cosmic rays, but when these winds weaken a bit, more cosmic rays get through, and so more clouds accumulate above our heads. What a long journey just for us to get a little rain, I thought, not to mention a few poems, and I squeezed my eyes shut. I thought to myself, in any case, that my grandfather's immigration form, which I keep with me in my wallet as if it's my own identity card, and sometimes do in fact present when I'm required to show a form of identification, was actually mine, that as a matter of fact I was born in August 1934 and not in April 1970. My grandfather, who didn't know his exact birthday, decided that he'd celebrate it on August 14th, the day he left Warsaw, and so he did, until he stopped, because of certain circumstances, which we will get into later on, but he eventually went back to celebrating it each and every year, and sometimes twice a year, until the day he died. From time to time he'd be reminded of the boat in which he came to Israel, and the day before his death he stood on the balcony of the Laniado Hospital and said to me, there's the shore. Those lights, so close. We'll anchor tonight. And he tossed a thick rope outside. They crossed the Mediterranean at summer's end, lay on the deck, and looked at the moon for lack of anything better to do. With each centimeter the boat progressed, I materialized a bit more, I myself drew closer and closer to existence. I wasn't on anyone's mind, but despite this, something was working at sea level and in the world in general, and I was the result. The captain, on the cabin roof at the stern of the ship, stood and aimed the ship's small telescope at the thin crescent without which—notwithstanding the ship and the water—it wouldn't have been possible to see, my grandfather told me, much of anything.

In preparation for the High Holidays, they would stuff our star maps behind the Holy Ark, and the astronomy class would take a month-long vacation. But the right edge of the map, the Andromeda and Pisces constellations, always poked out during services, since the star map was a bit wider than the width of the Holy Ark. No one noticed those little white points, but I knew that behind the Ark's inner curtain and plywood a bigger white point burned, by the name of Sirius, which was then the brightest star in the sky. Sirius, write Ward and Brownlee in *Rare Earth*, emits almost all its rays in the ultraviolet spectrum, whereas our sun emits only about ten percent of its energy as UV. Were it to emit more, we would be annihilated instantly, because even the little it does emit, that ten percent, is enough to burn our skin each summer. I imagined the wave of unseen rays emitted from Sirius bursting forth from the Holy Ark and striking us all, until my grandfather approached the Ark to close the curtain and thus cut short my thoughts. Someone went up to him and put his mouth to my grandfather's alert ear. I heard the echo of Yiddish, like a voice in a cave. My grandfather was being asked to replace the usual shofar blower, who hadn't shown up; it was only now, close to the appointed hour, that anyone had noticed. No one else dared touch the shofar, whose strong and unpleasant odor I remember well. The shofar, that curling horn, like a huge and yellowish fingernail, lay resting on a dark blue piece of velvet, on which all eyes were fixed during the silence that now prevailed in the synagogue. They were scared to look directly at the thing itself. My grandfather froze for a moment, wiped the sweat from his brow with a handkerchief bearing the National Health Service logo, and approached the horn. He extended his hand, lightly touched the gold-embossed letters embroidered onto the velvet, and then tapped his fingernail on the shofar itself, as if checking its solidity. The sound of this tap, like a ram crashing into another ram, echoed in the small space of the synagogue. My grandfather then turned his eyes toward the congregation, the large congregation, the beautiful congregation, raised the shofar to his lips, puffed out his cheeks, and blew into its narrow mouthpiece. Not a sound. I stared at the edge of the star map, my eyes glazing over. A yellow light poured into the synagogue, and an absolute, oppressive silence prevailed. The sound of the air blown through my grandfather's lips into the shofar was heard by those sitting at our table, which was the central table, but the rest of the synagogue probably heard nothing. Pffffff. My grandfather's face went red, the intertwined veins in his neck swelled up, but no sound came forth, as if the shofar were plugged up. The smell of fasting hung thick in the synagogue. An old man coughed and promptly collapsed. Gray brimmed hats began fanning his face and a flask with a potent smell was brought up to his nose. The old man revived at once and rose back to his chair, as if floating up from the bottom of the sea—a simple student's chair, the sort I sat on during our astronomy lessons. From the women's section, from the hungry women's dry mouths, rose a single thought, the desire for just a little weak, sweet tea in a tiny glass. My grandfather put down the shofar and reached for another, shorter shofar. His neck was drenched in sweat. With all his strength and with eyes closed he tried again, but no blast came from the shorter shofar either. Another old man crumbled and fell. The heat had become unbearable, even though it was raining out. My grandfather stood there with the horn in his mouth, it looked like some kind of shell, but finally he surrendered. He removed it from his lips, placed it carefully on the velvet next to the longer shofar, and then opened his mouth wide to swallow some air. The two synagogue wardens quickly grabbed hold of him from both sides a moment before he lost consciousness. "Water," someone yelled. But no water was brought, of course.

The next day everyone was informed—I was told about the thing only the following Rosh Hashanah—that the regular shofar blower had passed away on the evening of Yom Kippur, on his way home from Kol Nidrei prayers. On this Yom Kippur he heard no shofar blast, the warden said, and my grandfather answered, Yes, he heard the shofar from on high. His funeral took place the next day, but my grandfather was laid up in bed and did not attend, even though this same shofar blower had been his friend since childhood and indeed had immigrated with him on the very same ship, in August 1934, and in possession of, my grandfather told me many years later, *The Communist Manifesto* in Yiddish and three ancient shofars.

. . .

In *Rare Earth*, on the cover of which is an illustration of the planet Earth billions of years ago, covered in boiling lava and a small number of rocks, with a giant moon rising over the horizon to illuminate the bacteria that perhaps existed then in the depths of the sea, it's written that were the ratio between land and sea on Earth reversed—that is, were land to make up two-thirds of the Earth's surface and not one-third, as it is in actuality; or were the amount of water in the Earth's oceans distributed differently, that is, in deep, narrow shafts rather than horizontally, making up those great, wide liquid surfaces—life on earth would not be possible. This bit of information, and others like it, disturbed me during the days I was reading the book, and because of this disturbance I went out and lay down on the bench that same night, at the conclusion of which night I went home to write these words. In order for our lives to exist, says *Rare Earth*, we must be positioned at the proper distance from the sun and its heat, a distance at which water can remain in a liquid state, but that's not all—it's not only the distance from the sun that matters, but the mass of the sun as well, so that it won't send out too many damaging rays, on the one hand, and can keep us in a stable orbit around it without, at the same time, burning us to a crisp, on the other; the mass of the Earth too is vital, since it has to be large enough to maintain its atmosphere and oceans, yet not so big that its gravity would prevent us from being able to lift our feet or hands or a pen or a prayer book; and then, in order for us to be able to live, there has to be the right proportion of oxygen in the atmosphere, not too much and not too little, not to mention the fact that this perfect proportion of oxygen to other gasses had to appear at precisely the right moment in the history of planet Earth, at the very moment in which our lungs had developed and began to cry out for it, at the moment, I mean, when we first had any lungs at all. Without the right proportion of oxygen, lung-bearing creatures wouldn't have been able to evolve, and so we wouldn't have been able to evolve ourselves. In order for life to have evolved in this solar system, it had to be located in a galaxy suitable to such evolution, a galaxy in which there were enough heavy elements. The solar system needed to be neither too small nor elliptical, and its position in the galaxy neither too central nor too marginal. We needed a large moon as well. You could extend the list of requirements until this book's last page, and in fact to infinity; the absence of even one of them would have been enough, I saw, to destroy our world. At first this was a small, intellectual concern, but then it grew worrisome, threatening, like a headache or a toothache you have to bear from morning till evening. With each page of *Rare Earth*, the picture became clearer to me. I crossed the street and everything appeared unreal. I rested my hand on tree trunks; I drank cold water and stared at my cup in amazement. I wrote a sentence and immediately placed my pen on the almost empty page, and I thought of a strip of dry land in the middle of a round, tempestuous ocean. In order to be able to breathe the air, the authors of *Rare Earth* tell us, the creatures living on the face of planet Earth had to acclimate to the poisonous and deadly gas we call oxygen. The proportion of oxygen in the air rose quite quickly, from a trivial amount to twenty-one percent, and any species failing to adapt to this were doomed to destruction. This was a mass extinction, and we were drawn from it and live within it. I walked to the end of Smuts, on the night from which these lines arose, and all at once found myself asphyxiating from a lack of carbon dioxide. The pure oxygen scorched me. I turned red like a bar of rusty metal. I collapsed on my bench with the book *Rare Earth* in my hand, and I immediately knew what I would have to write. I lay oxygen-struck on the bench next to the synagogue, like a giant fish with hand-shaped fins. "Every atom in our bodies," write Ward and Brownlee, "resided inside several different stars before the formation of our sun . . . Planets, stars, and organisms come and go, but the chemical elements, recycled from body to body, are essentially eternal." Every atom in our bodies bounced around worlds at the edge of the universe. We were there, all of us, but we don't remember it. On the nail of my right big toe there is material from the great Eagle Nebula 5,900 light years away, and when I trim my nail the edges of the nebula fall into the toilet and are washed out to the Mediterranean Sea, where the fish eat them. The house of my grandfather, Zvi Burstein, 25 Dizengoff Street in Netanya, a short walk from the synagogue at Remez House, was also built from imported materials, or, to be more precise, stones from four European capitals: Berlin, Paris, Warsaw, and St. Petersburg. My grandfather and grandmother's residence was built by my father's grandfather, my great-grandfather, Shlomo Goldring. This was the first hotel in Netanya, Hotel Tel Aviv, which today would be considered a small hotel, but in the early thirties of the previous century was one of the city's most noteworthy structures. The hotel, which remains standing on a small limestone hill at the time of this writing, mainly served officers of the British Mandate. The municipality neither preserves nor destroys it, a policy in fact that would enable the writing of these lines, I thought. You should send a letter of thanks to the city of Netanya, I thought, half awake and half asleep, get up now and write an official letter of thanks to the city of Netanya, I said to myself. The stones for the hotel were transported from the port of Tel Aviv and arranged in four piles at the corners of the empty lot. Goldring approached the piles and declared in celebration: Berlin! Paris! Warsaw! St. Petersburg! And he placed the palm of his hand on each pile, as if through the power of touch he traveled for a moment to those distant cities, where he had spent so many years and whose languages he knew. In fact, Goldring, whom my father still calls "The Old Man," so I'll call him this as well, or rather his fortune, supports our family to this very day, one hundred years after those distant handshakes with distant merchants in German, French, Polish, and Russian. The Old Man wandered between the four piles of stones like a man treading a soft rug in which a map of the world had been woven. Eventually it became clear that the building supplier had deceived the Old Man and that all the stones had been brought from one source—Egypt, apparently. Hotel Tel Aviv had four floors—the German floor, the French floor, the Polish floor, and the Russian floor. With the German invasion of Prague, a few years after construction was complete, the Old Man changed the name of the German floor to the Czech floor. The stones for that floor, he told visitors, were brought specially from Prague. I myself, he said, went there to select them. Czech stone is the best stone of all, he declared. The British officers nodded politely and slid their hands along the walls, as if feeling for this difference in quality. He led them to the "English Room," which featured a flag of the United Kingdom and a giant King James Bible, a yard and a half in length, which lay there on a special lectern my grandfather had built for it, as well as an old "His Master's Voice" gramophone, and single-sided 78s, bearing one song each, for example "My Girl Will Sail the Thames," or "Richard, Richard, What've You Got At Downing Street," and a map of the Crown's colonies, which covered almost an entire wall, three meters high, and it's still there, dust covering all those abandoned countries, left to their fates with all their natural resources plundered. Which is why, even today, I seem to have an undue amount of reverence for the words *The Crown*. When a sun reaches old age it expands; the crown slips to one side, falls, and rolls silently along the kingdom's infinite marble floors, running over everything in its path. Such suns, as I'm sure you know, are called "red giants," and *Rare Earth* points out that without these red giants there would be no carbon in the universe, and without carbon, once again, our lives would not be possible, not to mention the sharpened tips of our pencils, crammed full of carbon from distant stars. In astronomy class, I pictured the Old Man as a sort of red giant with a giant red nose, driving in an old truck to Kfar Tavor, before he left there for Netanya, loaded with cupboards aplenty and three grandfather clocks, one of which still ticks in my parents' house in Netanya and disturbs the neighbors' sleep when it strikes midnight. I never saw the Old Man myself, he died five years before I was born, but his presence is certainly still felt in the many furnishings originating with him that are now scattered across the family space, including my apartment on Smuts. My writing desk is the Old Man's writing desk and his drawers are my drawers, and rare is the week I don't find at the back of one of these some tiny account book, or postage scale, or an old, blurry stamp. The drawers are deeper than my arms are long, and so I bend over, reach out a hand, and grope around in the dark until I find something. And sometimes, having found it, I leave it inside. I eat with the Old Man's fork and fill his pipe with hundred-year-old tobacco; I clean his pipe with his pipe cleaner, and I ride to the university on his bicycle: there you have my life in a nutshell. Without carbon there can be no life, and without red giants there can be no carbon. And this is the reason, apparently, why there wasn't life as we know it in the universe for hundreds of millions of years. It was necessary for it to wait for the first stars to come into being and then slowly expand and explode; it was like a building site still missing a single material, cement let's say, but the only cement around comes from a factory whose owner hasn't even been born yet. So the workers sit and wait until the parents of the man who will be the factory owner meet, and they anxiously follow the pregnancy until he's born, and wait out his youth until the critical moment he says to himself: Akiva, listen! A cement factory! Not a bad idea! And he sets up the factory and supplies the builders with the needed cement and doesn't know a thing about all the long years they waited, that they grew old in the meantime, how often their patience nearly ran out. That's how it was with carbon. You wait and at last it comes. Every wall in this hotel, claimed my father's grandfather, comes from four different cities. There's no telling the difference, the stones all touch one another. The Prague stone is up against the St. Petersburg stone, and the Paris stone kisses the Rome stone. Sometimes he'd get confused and mention other cities as well. We have a wonderful room vacant on the Madrid floor, he'd say, peering down anxiously at the reservation book, to a guest who happened to arrive by chance. And the crown nearly slipped off his head onto the open book.

When I was still just three and a half, and for reasons to be detailed later, the hotel—long ago the most elegant structure in Netanya and today a ruin at the top of a limestone hill—began to collapse inward, like certain types of stars, which converge in on themselves, growing more and more dense. The sea encroached upon the land, moving east, digging into the limestone slope until it reached the hotel's deep foundations. First the roof fell in on the Florence floor, then the shed in the eastern courtyard collapsed, and the orange tree next to the shed simply disappeared one day, as if it had never been—just like the pomegranate orchard that had been there well before the hotel was built. The massive poinciana tree that blazed in the front courtyard for sixty or seventy years collapsed in on itself as well, then disappeared after a few years, roots and all. A liquidation sale was announced, but no one bought a thing and nothing was sold. Only counterfeit coins changed hands, and the change received was in counterfeit coins as well. The crown was taken down and turned into a can-opener, and strands of hay were attached to the scepter, which was used to sweep up the abandoned paths leading to the hotel from Independence Square and Founders Square and from the central bus station and from the port of Netanya. A new iron lock was hung on the front doors. The lock rusted out overnight. Only one guest, or rather tenant, named Shimon, stayed on in the hotel by virtue of an old Ottoman law. He was so thin he had no need for the key, which my father keeps in his wallet with all his change. When he goes back to his room in the hotel at sunrise, he turns sideways and squeezes through the iron bars, straight into the corridor, which is where he sleeps.

. . .

Shimon is a black hole. In his youth his mass grew so dense that there was only one possible end for him. Had his diameter been a couple million times bigger, it wouldn't have happened. For sure. But at a diameter of four centimeters, the equation was straightforward. One morning he woke up, and it was over and done with. People thought he'd disappeared—that is, ceased to exist—but he knew well, from browsing through books on popular science, that it's impossible to disappear. And he knew he had become what is categorized as a micro black hole. Not a monstrous abyss whose width can't be measured, gaping and beating like a dark heart in the center of this and every galaxy, but really more of a black creature, quite small, unseen, inconsequential by cosmic standards, a file containing just one sheet of paper in an archive without end.

Actually, most of him didn't change. He knew from science books that he'd maintained his mass, no matter how it looked. He'd merely taken on such a great density that, all told, light could no longer escape him. Light, and, of course, anyone who got too close. Sad, really. But he had no control over it. The moment people crossed a certain threshold, they would spin toward him and be swallowed up like water down a bathtub drain. You could see them spin for a moment in the light, whirlpools of themselves. After that, well, when they would approach him during the day, no one would even notice that they'd vanished. But at night, a sort of yellow light would emanate from them briefly, like the light seen in telescopic photographs taken of the center of active galaxies. Their voices would be swallowed up a little more slowly than their images, but swallowed they were—not even the chirping of birds was immune. And birds had chirped over his head for years, in the old days.

But for the most part, no one went near him. For years he was forgotten. To tell the truth, people had always kept their distance even before he became a black hole. In a few years, he thought, I'll approach one of the space agencies, I'll donate my body to astrobiological science. He even started composing a will, consulting—through correspondence—with scientists. In the meantime, he's sitting on his bed—a bed or a borderless vacuum, hard to tell from this vast distance—waiting for night to descend. The stars calm him a bit, give him a feeling, despite his tragic fate, that he's a part of a great, sound, stable order. Each night he raises the blinds and stares up at the massive clusters of other holes in the sky, those great space bats, which no one on Earth can see except for him. And he waves his hand at these dark spots, and they, without hesitation, wave back.

. . .

In the days before the evening when I lay on the bench, under the influence of the book *Rare Earth*, I began seeing in everything—in the flames of the stove, in the courtyard tree, in street cats, in my teeth, my eyes, the sun, in the water flowing from the faucet, in the hair growing on my arms—something unreasonable, bizarre, and terrifying. I couldn't help it. Strange dreams came to me, for example the dream in which I purchased with a large bill a diamond as gray as a lead eye. I looked at the moon and immediately saw in it the light of the sun, just as I saw in the light of the sun the moon swimming in the sun's atmosphere and staring over at it incessantly. We all live in the sun's atmosphere. Reading *The Chilling Stars* by Svensmark and Calder, I almost passed out when I got to that piece of information. Even the simplest acts, like showering, reminded me that within the vast range of possible temperatures in the universe, from the freezing to the very hot, the range of temperatures possible on the face of planet Earth is tiny—less than forty degrees between the lowest and highest recorded temperatures in Tel Aviv, when a slight deviation in either direction would wipe out almost all life on the planet, and the writing of literature pretty much before anything else, I thought while soaping up. On my bench—the moon had already slipped behind a cloud and was now covered up by it—I tried to imagine writing these lines in a world where the temperature was a uniform seventy degrees Celsius, or even one hundred. In the depths of the seas, close to vents on the ocean floor emitting a type of black smoke-water, writes Peter Ward in his book *Life as We Do Not Know It*, temperatures over three hundred degrees Celsius have been recorded, and life has been found in these conditions, which everyone had previously believed was impossible. I dove down to these vents, in utter darkness, with pressure building in my ears. The needle gradually rose and settled on three hundred degrees Celsius, which, by the way, is nothing compared to the heat that will consume planet Earth when the sun expands—like a great conflagration devouring a speck of dust in its path. An author sitting in a sauna could write, at most, a short introduction to his book, perhaps a dedication, thanking his wife, the homemaker: "While I labored diligently over the research to this book, lapping up archival honey, you squatted, my dear Yocheved, under the weight of your knitting." Or else, it's possible a poet could write a short poem in a sauna, but a relatively long narrative like the one I'm writing here doesn't make sense in a sauna, and will never be written in a sauna, wet or dry. After fifteen minutes in a sauna you're barely awake, and you're lucky if you don't collapse from dizziness on your way past the soda machine. And here we're talking about a locked sauna, a sauna from which there is no escape. The temperature in Tel Aviv in the summer of 2009, when I'm writing all this, is almost thirty degrees Celsius during the evening hours, and the humidity is high, but still, I can breathe without difficulty. The percentage of oxygen in the atmosphere isn't measurably higher or lower than in recent years; asteroids ten kilometers in diameter haven't smashed directly into Tel Aviv; no neutron stars have exploded anywhere in our galaxy, eradicating every bit of life in Tel Aviv; and the sun hasn't become a red giant. It's true that human beings must live their lives in this insane pollution, which will one day be the end of us all, or of our offspring, who are for all intents and purposes still "us," but most human beings don't understand this, and routinely concoct the selfsame poisons they'll hand down to their grandchildren and great-grandchildren to drink. We were given a rare opportunity, and, probably, we'll blow it like idiots. Since 2007, the world population of bees has gone down by a third, but almost no one seems to have noticed. People lick up honey without understanding what honey is. Billions of bees disappeared within a few years, after approximately one hundred million years of this species' unbroken existence. Without bees there can be no flowers and no flowering plants. Approximately ten thousand plant species will disappear from the Earth if there are no bees around, as Maurice Maeterlinck wrote in his book, *The Life of the Bee*, adding that it was quite clear the damage resulting from this extinction wouldn't stop with the plant world, for, in his words, all is interwoven in this world of mystery. Were human beings to know that the moon hanging over their heads is what guarantees their existence, since without the moon, for example, the slant of the Earth's axis in relation to the sun would change such that sometimes the poles would face the sun and at times the equator—a cyclical sort of somersaulting that in the long term, over millions of years, would certainly wipe out all life on our planet, and in the short term would make living here difficult to the point of being unbearable—were human beings to realize this, perhaps they would go back to bowing down to the moon every night, spending their evenings staring at their benefactor from balconies built especially for this purpose, instead of watching, for example, a bunch of game shows. In the hotel built by the father of my grandmother there was a moon balcony just like this, crescent-shaped. We would sit there at dusk and gaze at the moon above, preferably full, preferably white, preferably behind a faint cloud. And it would rise and glimmer before our eyes. Once my grandfather bowed down to the moon, at the time of the Santification of the Moon, even though there are no instructions to do so. The synagogue warden reprimanded him and tried to pull him back to his feet with the help of the shofar blower, but he bowed down again without saying a word. He had no interest in astronomy, as I already mentioned, he even refused to look through telescopes. Also, he would only sit on the moon balcony in order to please my grandmother, and this poetess who used to stay at the hotel for free. But this time he bowed himself down before the moon, all the way to the floor, and bowed once more and rose, his forehead filthy, then continued reading the prayer with all of the congregation from the last pages of the prayer book for the High Holidays. The moon is the weight stabilizing the slant of planet Earth's axis, thus creating the seasons, the authors of *Rare Earth* point out. The winter is the moon's winter, autumn is the moon's autumn. People say "autumn," but they don't say "thanks to the moon"; people say "summer's here!" but they never take the moon into consideration. Without the moon's gravity and Jupiter's gravity and the sun's gravity, we don't survive, I thought, and sat up with some effort on the bench, because my back was already hurting from too much lying on hard wood. Without the moon, these pages would burn or freeze, just like their readers and the writer himself, I thought, and this thought caused me such unease that I started trembling there on the bench, like someone with a sudden fever. In my imagination I saw these pages coming together into a book and the book being published, but the next image was one of mass extinction, all the animals and plants on Earth, an event resembling any one of the at least fifteen extinctions our planet has experienced, extinctions no one seems to care about, aside from a few scientists. The existence of each and every thing on the land and in the sea required fifteen billion years, infinite years in fact, of preparatory work. Fifteen billion years of our universe's existence, to the best of our knowledge, were required in order for a corncob to appear, and we toss the corncob into the garbage and then go out and start a world war. The human civilization we're familiar with, according to *Rare Earth*, has come about in the space between two ice ages, the last ending in approximately 10,000 BCE, and the next of which will probably begin in a few thousand years. Yet, in the window of opportunity humans have enjoyed, a window with an exceptionally comfortable and stable climate, they've done everything in their ability to ruin this gift they've received. The window is liable to close, but no one thinks about this. Another factory, another jet, another pizza, another tank, another plastic knickknack, another book in hardcover. You look at the Yarkon River and your heart shrinks with sadness. For approximately fifteen billion years, a force that has no name toiled over this river, creating it from scratch, and here we return to our homeland and within twenty years spoil and poison the river. My grandfather stopped smoking his foul-smelling cigarettes back in the days when he was working at the National Health clinic—after leaving his job as an independent carpenter—at the very moment he read in a Health Service pamphlet about how, were it not for our atmosphere, we would be bombarded by various destructive rays, such as the infamous gamma ray, which would eradicate life on Earth within seconds and pave the way for ultraviolet rays to come down and gobble up the corpses too. We must sing a song of praise to our atmosphere and not do anything that's liable to be interpreted as showing it any disrespect, my grandfather said, after I read him a few pages about the atmosphere and the ozone layer from my astronomy notebook. The atmosphere is like a skin for us, and whoever smokes scorches the skin, my grandfather thought aloud; yet in the months that followed, I knew he still smoked in the bathroom, thinking no one saw him, but his cigarette smoke snuck out the window facing the courtyard where I played. He wanted to toss his last pack of cigarettes into the garbage when he went to work at the Um Khalid clinic—which was erected on the site of a Palestinian village, whose inhabitants were expelled or fled in fear and were not allowed to return at the end of the War of Independence, and whose name we would conjure up each time one of us got the flu, and we would all troop out to the Palestinian village Um Khalid without ever suspecting that the Um Khalid clinic was, in fact, the Palestinian village Um Khalid—wanted to throw them away for good in order to show his good faith and be given medicine and get better, but he backed down from his decision and instead gave the pack to the head doctor at Um Khalid, a man who smoked cigarettes from morning to night and even blew the bitter smoke onto his many sick patients out of belief that the smoke would disinfect them and so exterminate the bacteria they were drenched in and which was eating the better part of their bodies. This doctor, it became clear later on, was a submarine mechanic impersonating a doctor, and a surgeon at that, for the sake of prestige. Amazingly, he managed to heal more than a few seriously ill people, though one or two patients ended their lives under his scalpel. Anyway, my grandfather bequeathed his final pack to this man, coughed a bit, and carried on with his work. The world is full of diseases and some go ahead and add smoking to their many troubles. They bury their dead and smoke by the cemetery wall, next to the mourning notices, blowing smoke into the eyes of the gravediggers, lighting up cigarillos during the week of mourning while still invoking the name of the deceased and of the lung disease that, eventually, vanquished him, while still secretly smoking a last cigarette in the bathroom next to his room in the hospital and gasping along to their own deaths. My lawyer neighbor passed by the bench again with his dog, and while bending down to pick up an enormous pile of feces with his bare hands, he offered me a cigarette, which I declined after a moment's hesitation, and I even held my breath as he continued polluting the air of the boulevard with his words and the smoke of the Gauloises cigarettes he had shipped especially from Lyons. Fifteen billion years of work, work without which this boulevard and the trees planted along it would not have been even remotely possible, and here he is smoking Gauloises like it all has nothing to do with him. But there's no need to go back fifteen billion years, twenty thousand will do. At the end of *Rare Earth*, it says that twenty thousand years ago, at the height of the last ice age, a rare type of star called a magnetar exploded twenty thousand light years away from us, that is at a distance of approximately 200,000 trillion kilometers, seemingly about as far as you can get, but actually right next door, if you consider a star's rays to be extensions of the star. The magnetar grew until it was tapping on our porch window, and then it broke the window. A magnetar is a highly dense star, wickedly dense I would say, if that meant anything. An explosion, or some other disturbance, in this star sent gamma rays on a twenty-thousand-year journey of destruction. For twenty thousand years the rays paddled through the darkest of dark, without tiring, until they reached us on August 27, 1998, flooding us like a wave for five minutes, breaking every measuring device we've got. August 27, 1934, was my grandfather's first day at the Immigrant Center, and on that day the magnetar's deadly rays were still quite far away. During the thirties, numerous Jews arrived here from Europe, and there's no need to mention that they fled from Hitler and all his jolly collaborators. If it weren't for his searing speeches—the man would sweat so much during every speech that twenty liters of cold mineral water were needed to revive him, Hitler that is, writes Ian Kershaw in his biography—if it weren't for his speeches, it's fair to say that my grandfather would have stayed in Europe. But on a trip to Germany in the early thirties, my grandfather happened upon one of the rallies at which Hitler spoke, which was held in the front courtyard of the Alte Pinakothek (a museum where I worked as a night watchman for a year) and saw up close the abundance of sweat pouring out of Hitler during the speech. The literary fashion in Germany during those years, as Sebastian Haffner tells it in *Defying Hitler: A Memoir*, and as my grandfather told me himself, was to write books about childhood memories, family novels, stories of children's summertime frolics, as Haffner says, and "spiritual" and "timeless" books of all sorts. But no childhood memories, writes Haffner, could serve as a defense. These terrifying books, like the rivers of sweat my grandfather saw opposite the museum, and not the contents of Hitler's speech, are what persuaded him, so he told me many times, to return immediately from Germany to Poland and pack his things. Facing his gaping suitcase he tried to convince his three brothers and parents of the reality of the danger as well. You don't understand, he said, the man sweats liters of sweat during a single speech, a man like that is dangerous, the sweat testifies to this as well as a thousand witnesses. Yet they were unwilling to believe that real danger could be hidden inside that young statesman, and they also dismissed the descriptions of his sweating as hyperbole. Even the regulations my grandfather showed them in print, forbidding Jews to put their hands in their pockets and whistle the "Ode to Joy" from Beethoven's Ninth Symphony, they treated as entirely insignificant. So what reason would a Jew have to put his hands in his pockets now anyhow? Two years later my grandfather arrived in the Land of Israel, and in August, when he was sent to work in the orchards of Ra'anana and became dehydrated, he recalled that same speech in Munich. Ever since, Hitler's murderous perspiration would pass before his eyes each summer. He saw it all in that sweat. I was so close, he said, that I could have touched him, there in his sweat-soaked uniform and with those scented handkerchiefs that he used to wipe the sweat off his forehead and his neck, handkerchiefs he would pull out of his pocket one after another, sometimes fifty or sixty scented silk handkerchiefs at a single rally.

On August 27, 1998, when the magnetar rays struck earth, my grandfather, like every year on this date, went back over the August 27, 1934 issue of the *Davar* newspaper, which he kept from those first days in the Land of Israel. In that issue, which came into my possession after he passed away, the following incidents were reported: Avigdor Jacobson was brought to his final resting place and the high commissioner sent his condolences; one of Mosley's anti-Semitic gatherings was scheduled to take place in September, in London; the debts of the Jewish Agency and Jewish Foundation Fund had been reduced; investigations into the abduction of a girl from Hayarkon Street were ongoing; talk of an Anglo-Japanese alliance were gaining strength; Dr. Killian Bloom, an expert on diseases of the nerves and spirit (psychological therapy, psychoanalysis) had moved from Berlin (and here was a large blank space in the announcement, as if to illustrate this dramatic journey) to Jerusalem and was now receiving patients in his clinic on Prophets Street, opposite Hadassah Hospital, between the hours of ten to twelve in the morning, telephone number 1645, and it even gave a home address, which was apparently by a tennis court; while in Berlin, the city Dr. Bloom left, Dr. Lazarus Goldshmidt had translated the last three volumes of the Talmud into German. Many years later, my grandfather told me in 1998, I went to see that same Dr. Bloom in Jerusalem, in 1974 or 1975, when I thought I couldn't take it anymore. Here in Netanya I had no one to turn to. According to my calculations then, if in 1934 the doctor was twenty or thirty years old, he would still be practicing his profession. I put the newspaper in my pocket and traveled to Jerusalem. Clearly the old, four-digit phone number was no longer in service, but I thought perhaps he was still receiving patients at his clinic on Prophets Street, across from Hadassah Hospital, even though Hadassah Hospital was no longer on Prophets Street. At the worst, I'll have a walk around Jerusalem, he said. Sometimes a man wants to walk around Jerusalem, to go down to the street next to the Jerusalem Theater at five in the afternoon. Sometimes you hear the word Jerusalem or read about Jerusalem in a book of Agnon's set in Jerusalem, my grandfather said to me. Actually, all of Agnon's stories are set in Jerusalem, he said. And you're already sitting on the express bus to Jerusalem. On Friday at five o'clock, six o'clock in Jerusalem, he said, you feel like you have a chance. So I went on foot from the station to Dr. Bloom's private apartment in Rahavia, on Abarbanel Street, and I searched for the tennis court mentioned in the announcement. And there actually was a tennis court, and next to it, in the shade of some large trees, a man in a three-piece suit sat petting a dog. He asked me if I was looking for Professor Bloom, and I said, Yes, I'm looking for him. If so, the Professor is in Switzerland now, said the man in the suit. Every August he vacations in St. Moritz with his son, and sometimes, when his son's condition deteriorates, he extends their stay until springtime. My grandfather asked, from the other side of the tennis court's fence: And you, would you be able to help me? The man looked at his racquet for a long time and said sadly: No.

. . .

In his book *The Call of Distant Mammoths*, Peter Ward writes that most mammals from the last ice age, which came to an end around 10,000 BCE, went extinct because of early man, who hunted the mammoths and the mastodons, just as we, their descendants, hunt the descendants of the mammoths and the mastodons—the elephants. I closed my eyes and recalled a dream from a few days earlier. In my dream I entered a large house to visit a well-known Italian art collector who lives in Tel Aviv. To my surprise, the walls of his house were bare, and hundreds upon hundreds of rectangles and squares in the dust on the walls indicated the places where pictures had recently hung. Here and there in this beehive of empty quadrangles a picture remained that they had forgotten to remove or didn't want to take. Everything pre-twentieth century, the collector, who sat on a bed in a room crowded with furniture, said to me, *she* took. And he described his divorce trial and all the fighting over property. He, who'd built the collection, he said, albeit with his wife's money . . . but I was no longer listening, as my eyes wandered over the fields of rectangles stretching in every direction. On my bench I opened my eyes and recalled a story about the scientist Frank Drake, mentioned in *Rare Earth*. In 1974 he broadcast a radio communication toward a star cluster, because he hypothesized that the chance was high someone there would receive it, due to the density of suns inside it. He knew that the broadcast wasn't likely to reach its destination for another 20,000 years, but he did this with all the decisiveness of a man writing a book that he knows will be published in a year or two. You write books and direct them to the right place, as it were, and the years pass, but no word comes back to you. It doesn't come because the message hasn't arrived yet, and the message hasn't arrived yet because of the distance involved. Yet, somewhere another person sits and listens, night after night, for just such a message, and when yours reaches him, his instruments will flicker. The message must arrive, the message always arrives eventually. There is someone awaiting word from you, don't disappoint him. In any case, it says in *Rare Earth* that today we know that Drake was mistaken, and that it's precisely because of the great density of suns in that star cluster that the chances of there being life there are insignificant. There can be no night in a star cluster, because suns surround you on all sides. Sunrises in every direction, sunsets in every direction, tens of thousands of sunrises and sunsets, I imagined. You can't hide from the light and thus can't hide from the powerful radiation. A supernova would eradicate all life up to a distance of thirty light years around the exploding star. A long way, indeed, but so is the distance that radiation can travel from the explosion, and it's not impossible that such radiation is making its way toward us at this very moment, and will flood us with a blinding shower at noon tomorrow. Star clusters contain many young suns, while other points in the universe provide views of old galaxies that are starting to grow twisted and wrinkled, their beautiful, spiral forms, familiar to us from numerous photos, lost forever. In my dream, I passed between the collector's large rooms, wandering here and there and looking at the rectangles, most of them small, but a few of them very large, three meters wide, and the collector walked behind me and from time to time described what had been painted in the painting that had once covered this or that rectangle. And at times in the dust on the walls I could see remnants of the wide-open expanses, the clouds that once floated there, the gardens and the streams and the beautiful ruins, hidden almost entirely among the trees.

. . .

For many years I only saw straight ahead, and sometimes, for a moment, to the sides or behind. When I was lying on that bench, my gaze was forcibly raised skyward. Imagining writing these words, I pictured myself resting my notebook not upon the table but rather upon the sky. The words changed immediately. To my great surprise, the sky supported my notebook, however much the heavenly dome that ought to have spread out like an endless writing table was for the most part obstructed by the boulevard's trees and buildings and mainly by the air pollution and light pollution eating into the night like a heatless fire and preventing the light of most stars from reaching our eyes, already unaccustomed to being raised skyward. The night sky is an indictment against humanity. The night sky and each absent star will stand as cruel evidence at our trial. The level of carbon dioxide in the atmosphere is perpetually rising, writes Peter Ward in his book *Under a Green Sky*. According to one hypothesis, it began to rise with the beginning of agriculture, approximately ten thousand years ago, and with the industrial revolution a hundred and fifty or two hundred years ago the process sped up. Since then, the indictment against us has been coming together faster and faster. There are scientists, writes Ward, who predict that within three hundred years the ice in Greenland will melt, and after that Antarctica's ice will go too, and by the year 3,000 we'll have returned to the Eocene climate, which would mean, in today's terms, a catastrophe of enormous proportions and the end of human civilization in its present form. Excavations reveal that in the Eocene epoch there were palm and date trees in the Arctic Circle. Palm and date trees can only grow in climates where the reader will not be surprised to find, for example, our good friend, none other than the Anopheles mosquito and its permanent escort, malaria. But well before this point is reached, the surface of the oceans will rise and implement the verdict following our conviction at trial. Low lying, crowded countries will be the first to endure the punishment, which will eventually, and justly, reach every one of us. Millions of refugees from countries like Bangladesh, writes Ward, will begin a process whose end no one knows. In the Tel Aviv sky it is still sometimes possible to see isolated stars, but there are cities whose skies are entirely star free, and there the hangman is already polishing his tools and eating his breakfast, soft yellow butter on burnt zwieback. Nigel Calder and Henrik Svensmark have tried to cast doubt on these gloomy forecasts with their book *The Chilling Stars*, in which they argue that the cooling and heat-ing of planet Earth stems not from man-made changes to the level of carbon dioxide in the atmosphere, but rather from the cosmic rays that emanate from supernovas and so affect the clouds over our heads. When the solar winds—which curb cosmic rays, remember—weaken, many more of those rays reach us here on Earth, following which many more clouds form and the surface of the planet cools. I was cold on my bench, but I couldn't see any cosmic rays, so I wasn't going to be much use settling the scientists' argument. But I did recall a particular statement from Calder and Svensmark's book: "[W]e owe our existence . . . to lights no longer burning in the sky." That is, to stars that exploded and went out and whose radiation is washing over us millions of years after their death, like a letter from a rich uncle that circled the world ten times because of some miscalculation in postage. I myself received a letter like this, said my astronomy teacher during our class's first field trip, and when it reached me, many years after it was sent, I found a banknote inside that hadn't been in circulation for some time. We covered our eyes with soft blue handkerchiefs and got on a bus, holding each other's hands and laughing quietly. We traveled for about two hours with eyes covered and got off the bus with eyes covered. The teacher instructed us to lie on our backs and so we did, helping one another in silence to clear away the small rocks that we felt scattered on the ground. A moment later he instructed us to remove our blindfolds. We found ourselves in a cold and quiet place, perhaps in the Arava Desert, we guessed. It was cold and the teacher passed from one student to another and covered us with prickly wool blankets. I hid this blanket in my bag when we returned to Netanya the next morning, and it's still with me to this day, and I even had the opportunity to cover myself with it once, which perhaps I will describe later. Wrapped in the rough wool blankets, we lay on our backs and looked, for the first time in our lives, at a firmament packed with stars, that is, a normal firmament. It was wondrous, beyond our ability to take it all in, and that of our teacher too, though he had already seen this sky many times in actuality as well as in his dreams. The soles of our feet were all pointing toward a central spot, but our eyes darted in every direction. All of us, I thought years later, lying on the bench, must have looked like we were dead. No one moved and no one spoke. Every so often a "falling star"—that is, a meteorite—sliced across the sky. It was the month of August—the 11th, I believe—and the meteor shower in the Perseus constellation was at its annual peak. While lying on the bench, I asked myself if my grandfather, during his final days in Poland, also lifted his head above the suitcases he had packed and saw this meteor shower that has taken place for thousands of years each and every year on August 11th. It was a moonless night, in the desert, and after an hour of lying on the sand, scattered here and there in the clearing, the meteorites began to appear by the hundreds, like flocks of sparrows that sometimes dive-bomb low houses in the summertime. All of us had learned and knew well that meteorites are rocks burning up in the atmosphere and that the sight we were watching in amazement was nothing but the sight of a mass death, the death of rocks burning up at the end of a journey hundreds of thousands of kilometers long. At the same time, it was also life that we were seeing, our lives, which are spared again and again from their impact. Each "falling star" shows us our atmosphere protecting us and granting us life. The moon is evidence of the fate awaiting a heavenly body lacking protection. I imagined each meteorite in the shower falling and striking the head of one of us, the students of the Remez House astronomy class, and only our teacher surviving and returning alone to Netanya and standing empty-handed facing our families. The bus driver would be struck down as well, and the teacher himself would have to drive the big empty bus, and he would go the wrong way and arrive somewhere else, but his detour wouldn't be too extended so long as he could see the sky and the stars. There will be one crater for each student, yawning where each of us had lain, and the craters will be named after us. I saw my crater, too. Thus we lay for an hour or two on our backs. And then, while gazing at the triangle that is the tail of the constellation Leo, I fell asleep. I would have liked to record what I dreamt, but to be honest I don't remember it. Maybe the stars were my dream. We had all brought maps of the eastern stars along, but these never left our bags. Anyway, most of the constellations were lost among the tremendous abundance of points of light. Our telescopes too remained rolled up in a large blanket, inside the bus. It felt as though we were likely to remain there forever, on our backs, like prehistoric larvae, lacking armor, wooly to the touch, most of our eyes directed to the sky, barely moving, nourished by the light of the stars, our hearts beating calmly. We knew that we were seeing into the distant past, that the lights above us weren't shining now but rather shined hundreds of thousands or millions of years ago. Or, no. Really, it shines now and in the distant past all at once, as we knew, and this knowledge made us serene. It was already two or three in the morning. Someone got up to pee, and others got up after him. No one bothered to search for cover in the great darkness. I too stood up and peed in the cold, wrapped up in the blanket that I still have. I pictured how, on the other side of the mountains to the east, a giant, red, frightening moon would rise, the likes of which you only see in movies and science books. We returned in silence to the bus and sat down, each one in a seat for two. The driver had been asleep on the rear bench the whole time and didn't notice us entering. No one dared disturb him, so we lay on the seats and waited for dawn to wake him—and us as well, as it turned out. Last night's *Davar* newspaper was spread out over the driver's face, the ten nails of his bare feet pressed against the window, and his head was resting, I noticed only some time later, on the giant down blanket inside of which the telescopes had been rolled up.

. . .

A plastic bag fluttered down the boulevard and I, from my place on the bench, caught it and stuck it in the space between the planks. Plastic bags fly all over the city like terrestrial jellyfish, tens of thousands of plastic bags bearing the logos of supermarkets and publishers, and the day will come when they attack us and cover our heads and choke us; each man will suffocate in his own bag. I didn't come up with this sentence myself; no, I heard it, back at the end of the seventies, from the mouth of a neighbor who lived three stories above us on Bialik Street in Netanya. He was a friendly person and he taught me, among other things, the rules of chess, and also how to crack my toes, and a few other useful things to boot, such as how to make a free call from a public telephone. He was a painter, the neighbor from upstairs, and I remember a few paintings that he did in the style of Salvador Dali. On two walls in the entrance-

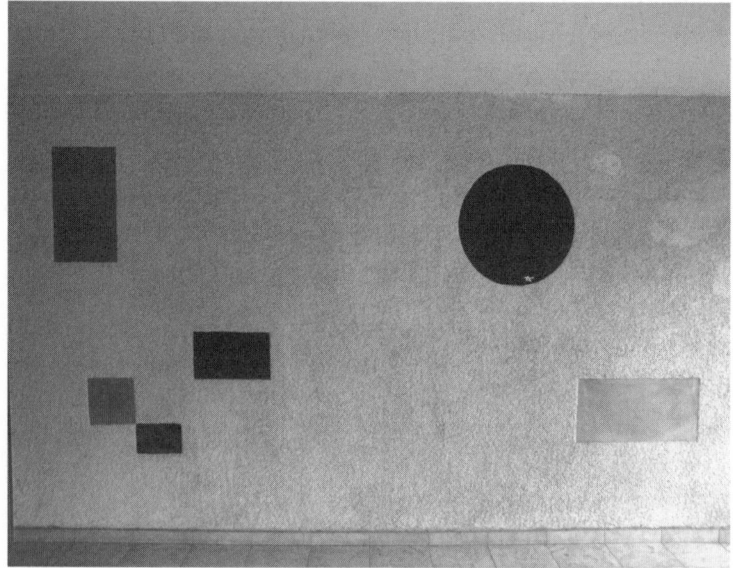

way to the building he painted murals made up of geometric shapes, right on the plaster, and they're still there. It could be that he made them in exchange for lower rent, I don't know. After he left the building, the tenants put up new mailboxes on one of the decorated walls, ruining a work of art. But a bit of the mysterious image still peeks over the metal boxes, like an alien of some sort. This glowing creature's face is hidden by a dark half circle, part giant smile and part deformed half moon, and above its head, outside the frame, a strange shape hovers, like a *Y* suspended magically in space. And every time we would open our mailbox we would peek inside to see a bit of the picture's lower section. But in the darkness of those deep mailboxes, we didn't see a thing.

The picture on the facing wall, a few rectangles and a single circle, is still unscathed. What the painting is meant to represent, if anything, I can't say. If this is a solar system, then in this solar system the plaster planets are rectangular: two brown ones and two gray ones to the left of their plaster sun, and a pale one to the right. For some reason the left side is the dark side, as those rectangles are dimmer, whereas the rectangle on the right looks illuminated, and then it's much closer to the plaster sun than the other rectangles. For many years when I was a kid, I would pass by this wall without so much as slowing down to contemplate it. Now, the mural looks to me like a coded roadmap to my future, or an astrological chart no one can decipher. The large space between the circle and the dark rectangle to the left bothers me in particular, and when I recently traveled to Netanya, a few weeks after that same night on the bench, in order to photograph this wall, I found myself leaning right up against the space, as though it were my own designated spot, as though I could step right inside. New tenants passed by and looked at me as if it was perfectly natural for a man to be standing there like that. Maybe they worried that I'd come down off the wall to harass them if they objected. So I stood there inside the wall and remembered.

Across the hall from my neighbor the painter, in the building on Bialik Street in Netanya, lived a Belgian man, Kligler was his name. He would save stamps for me from the many letters he received from Belgium and France, and in order to do this would soak the envelopes in warm bathwater. To whom he wrote and who wrote to him, I don't know. I can still see those envelopes in the bath. Afterward, he would stick the stamps to the faucet and the soap dish in order to dry them. I still have them, to this day. But it's not the Belgian neighbor who concerns me now, but rather the painter neighbor, whom I will call Fabian Zachariah. I loved this neighbor. I was certain there wasn't anything he didn't know how to do. He taught me "Scholar's mate" and other chess tricks you can do with the queen and the bishop, and even now I can still beat high-level players. Modesty aside, I'll say that I'm one of the better chess players in Hebrew literature; I once amazed S. Yizhar with a quick win at a competition held at the Gedera Community Center, and in an exhibition match held at the Carmel Center in Haifa, I beat A. B. Yehoshua who is, as everyone knows, a Grandmaster. My neighbor also gave me a brief tutorial in European art history, from Giotto to Dali, who was, in his opinion, the greatest painter. One time he sat me down next to him and quickly gave me a précis of the entire ecological system of our planet. He grabbed a piece of paper and drew in charcoal what is called the food chain and the water cycle, and afterward suggested I drink a glass of water and go to the bathroom to pee. This was about a week before he vanished without warning, a disappearance whose explanation became clear only a few weeks later. It turned out he'd kidnapped a boy and held him for ransom. According to his instructions, the money was to be placed inside a barrel in the middle of a field, and despite police surveillance, he popped out from a hiding place near the barrel, removed the sack of ransom money from it, and dissolved into the dark of night. He didn't free the abducted child, though, because by that time the boy was already dead. My neighbor had strangled the child in a car when he tried to call for help, at least that's what the investigation revealed. My neighbor buried the boy in the sands of Netanya and later led the police investigators to the site. When the police searched the area, they found a plastic bag hidden in a cinder block, inside of which was a can, the cover of a large sketchpad, a drawing pen, and a pair of thin nylon gloves. What the boy's final moments were like—his name in this book will be Shimon Oded—we won't ever know with certainty. Shimon Oded was my age, and the murderer's own children were my friends. I'm not certain what effect this incident had on my life, but it's clear to me now that were it not for that event, this book wouldn't have been written. My neighbor was caught when he tried to deposit the ransom, full of marked bills, into his bank account. During that same visit of mine to his apartment, before the kidnapping, when he suggested I go to the bathroom and urinate out the water I'd drank, as part of my lesson in ecology, I went, as he asked, but didn't pee. When I returned to the living room he said, now you are connected to the clouds and the sea, and he pointed up and down. Clouds-rain-water-urine-sea-clouds, he said, this is the entire system. If you understand that, you understand everything. And if I may illustrate it in a different way, he said, an ant walks on a path. The path is on the Earth. The whole Earth—the whole planet—holds up the ant, gives it a foothold. And who holds up the Earth? he asked and immediately answered: All of empty, infinite space holds up the earth. Understand? he asked, and I lied and said, Yes, I understand. There are children, he said, who don't understand. I explain it to them and they continue to waste resources, make a mess, throwing toilet paper into the bowl like it was nothing. There are clogs in the building every day. People need one square and use half a roll.

I'll mention a few more of our neighbors: the cosmetician Edith Weinberger (in whose apartment I saw my mother reclining on a chair, a white mask on her face, her two eyes covered with cucumber) and her husband Tiberius, who was named after the Roman Caesar Tiberius Claudius Nero; Mr. Movshovitz or Movshovich, who had a mustache and an old father; and Dr. Klugman from the ground floor, who once removed a sewing machine needle from my finger and claimed that he was fluent in the language of ants. But here I'm just avoiding the painter's apartment on the fifth floor and the kidnapping incident again. So I'll bring up just one more memory concerning that: When at my neighbor's request I went to the bathroom in his apartment, something caused me to continue walking down his hallway, which was identical to the hallway in our apartment on the building's second floor. The door to the bedroom at the end of the hallway was open a bit, and through it I saw something strange, like red or purple letters, illuminated and kind of hovering in the air. I went closer, and with fingers trembling I opened the door. On a large wall mirror was written, in lipstick or perhaps a paintbrush, these words: "To my dear wife Leah. Love you always. Fabian." I stood there a while, paralyzed with terror, until I noticed behind the letters my own head reflected in the mirror, and behind that the open door, and I turned around and left. I drew back my hands and retreated to the bathroom. I didn't manage to urinate. I counted to three and flushed the toilet. Only then did I return to the living room. My painter neighbor was still sitting there, bent over the chessboard, considering the arrangement of the pieces, tapping the tip of his finger on the mane of a white knight, mumbling, his eyes running across the squares, not at all noticing my return, murmuring to the heads of the pieces.

. . .

I believe that the child [   ] lives. The abductors did not kill him. As it is written in the Torah: "What profit is it if we slay our brother and conceal."
For at the meal at which they sat with their father Jacob our father, no
body touched bread. Until one broke out weeping.

(First stanza of Avoth Yeshurun's poem "A Great Miracle That You Made on Television," from his collection *Homograph*. The poem was written on the 11th of July, 1980. This was summer vacation of fourth grade.)

Three o'clock full of darkness each person with his things
Inside the hole he dug in the ground
It's possible to hear the snores impossible not to hear
The bombs falling far away
And after each fall a yellow light is seen in the distance
A multitude of yellows
Because I was the signaler I arranged the two-way for myself in the vehicle
A possibility to listen to the radio
Someone hit me on the back and said look out,
There are enemy units in the area
Take the driver and go to the command tent
And don't try to convey the message about the units on the two-way
Go
A large open trunk full of communication equipment
That is screaming at the peak of silence [. . .]
And the whole time the driver asking did you see anything did you see anything
Don't worry when I see them I'll kill them
I recalled the two-way that was tuned to the radio
Against all the orders I had received to maintain complete silence
I turned the knob as high as possible

(Yoram Kupermintz—*October—War Diary*, 10.9.1973)

. . .

My father stood at the pick-up station at the Hadera Junction. It was the Yom Kippur War. From a distance he made out the giant Dodge belonging to Moshe Kashti, the husband of my grandmother's sister, who was then the director general of the Ministry of Defense. Kashti stopped his American car and picked up my dad and they traveled in silence to Netanya. Tank transporters were taking up most of the road and so the trip went very slowly. From time to time Kashti pulled onto the shoulder to pass one of these. He broke the silence only once. He pointed at the radio, which was turned on and lit up but wasn't making a sound, and said, "The radio's broken." Again and again he pulled onto the shoulder, and again and again he honked out a warning when he pulled back onto the road. His massive car stuck out even among all the armored vehicles, and my dad told me years later that for a moment it seemed to him that he was watching their progress from above. Suddenly he fell asleep, and Kashti had to wake him up when they got to Netanya. He honked the horn in order to wake him. It still didn't help. He actually leaned on the horn, he said. He dropped my dad off on Bialik Street and drove from there to his house on Commanders Street in Tsahalah. Later on it became clear that he already knew. The thing had happened a few days before this, on the ninth of October. In the Defense Ministry they know before everyone. He knew but didn't tell my dad a thing. Because how could he have told him? In the car? After all, my dad fell asleep so fast, and could he have even managed to wake him to give him the news? When my dad finally woke up, before getting out of the car and saying farewell, he said, if we had a little time I could fix the radio for you, Moishe, but I haven't slept for two days, I don't want to break it, maybe another time, now I'm going to sleep and will wake up in November. The car took off and he saw my mother running toward the house from the direction of the hotel on Dizengoff Street, with me in her arms. I was three and half, and from her face, far away, from the end of the street really, he immediately understood what had happened. Immediately. And from my face as well.

. . .

It's hard to say how long I dozed on the bench. When I woke up, the moon was no longer there. I haven't worn a watch for years. When you're immersed in deep time, in eras and epochs and periods like the Mesozoic and the Jurassic and the Triassic, it's hard to pay attention to a watch, which declares with utter seriousness, for example, that it is now 8:10 A.M. The minute of 8:10, like any other minute, causes you to forget deep time, and I had already been sinking into deep time. I had sunk for example into the time of the Permian extinction, which took place approximately two hundred and fifty million years ago. This was when almost all life on planet Earth became extinct. Most people don't know about it. Perhaps this is for the best. Today is Rosh Hashanah 2009, the time is 8:48 A.M., and two hundred and fifty million years ago . . . I can't complete a sentence like that. But it must be possible to write a sentence like that, because that's reality, I thought then, on the bench, while searching in vain for the moon behind the rooftop water tanks.

I removed my red watch from my wrist after reading Peter Ward's book *The Call of Distant Mammoths* for the first time; it's about our fathers' fathers, upright man, who with primitive spears may have wiped out numerous animals, among them the great mammals of the ice age, the mammoths and the mastodons, or in any case contributed considerably to their extinction. All measuring devices fall apart in the face of data too great for them to process, and my watch no longer showed the time. My grandfather, by contrast, wore two watches. A watch on each wrist. One watch was metal, its glass face cloudy, its hands phosphorescent, and its tick-tock could be heard from a distance (when praying he would place it on the page in front of him, face down). His second watch was plastic, digital, stylish according to the terms of the late sixties. When he was asked the time—and he was asked the time again and again by the many sick people who would arrive early in the morning to grab a place in line at the National Health clinic—he would first check the old watch and afterward the new watch and come up with an average of sorts. The metal watch, my father recently told me, belonged to my grandfather's older brother, Yaakov, who was a soldier in the Polish army. A single postcard from Bialystok was received from him in the early forties; more than this nobody knows. The second watch belonged to his son, my uncle, my father's brother. His name was Shalom Burstein and he was killed in a tank in the Yom Kippur War. According to the official memorial books, my uncle was just about to be discharged from the army, and so I've seen the discharge papers that had already been issued to him, along with the reason for discharge: *completion of service*—but with the outbreak of war he went up to the Golan Heights and voluntarily rejoined his tank crew. He was killed while on pre-release vacation, on October 9, 1973, and two months later my brother, who is named after him, was born. For me my uncle's death in the war is tied, in ways I'll never be able to understand, to the conviction of my neighbor the painter from the fifth floor for kidnapping and murder, just as the gravity of both the moon and Jupiter delineate the path and life cycle of planet Earth, as these distant gravities meet in planet Earth, working together without knowing a thing about one another. A great, distant gravitational pull works just as well as a small and nearby one—that is the law. The death of my uncle when I was three and a half and the murder of that boy when I was eleven, my grandfather's watches, and the large German grandfather clock my parents still have—very slowly the borders of the net that envelops me are revealed, a very little bit of the net, the edges of the edges. I describe it as a net because the net enveloping me is the net enveloping everyone. The ends of my net are connected to the nets of every human being and of every thing. There is only one net. The grandfather clock and the moon are shared by all of us—therefore, literature is possible. All of these, my uncle's death, the boy's murder, my grandfather's watches, they are planets in my solar system or in what I could call my universe, which is in fact every person's universe, just as the universe of each person is my universe as well, just as the sun is part of the solar system but by the very same measure is part of a galaxy and a cluster of galaxies and the universe. I was not at the center of these things, but they had exerted their pulls on me just as I certainly had exerted mine on them. When my uncle went up to the Golan Heights to voluntarily rejoin his tank crew, perhaps he thought of me as he thought of the rest of my family. Once I dreamed that he carried my picture along, a bent Polaroid, like an amulet in the pocket of his uniform when he climbed into the tank, but I know, in the dream, that the amulet won't protect him, and the picture goes up in flames inside his pocket, bubbles spread across it like boiling blisters, but he doesn't notice the fire. In some sense I was in that tank, even if in another sense I was outside the tank. I was, my grandfather and grandmother were, my dad was. We sat crowded in the tank illuminated by a single light, and were silent. The soldiers hung an old calendar there and one date was circled on it. Sometimes we sat there together, all of us, shoulder to shoulder, and sometimes I was there alone. We hugged my uncle and he departed from us. They raised the iron hatch for us; we had to leave. We left, but we knew we'd return.

Once, after a class I taught in the Literature Department at Tel Aviv University, I went out to rest for a bit and looked for a quiet corner. I came upon a few stairs leading down and at the bottom of them a bit of a depression in the ground, a sort of small cement pit, which I had never noticed before, even though it was close to, almost right next to, the Gilman building where I've taught in recent years. A faded sign announced "memorial under repair." I went down the tiny stairs into the hole-memorial, and found posted there a memorial plaque from Tel Aviv University dedicated to the students who fell in the various wars. For some reason I recalled the Zen proverb, empty-handed I return home, which I mumble to myself from time to time. My uncle's name—he had in fact been accepted by the University's history department, and was supposed to begin his studies a few days after he was killed in October 1973—was engraved there along with all the others, and I noticed it immediately, in the rightmost column. I approached the wall. He was already registered, they explained to me later in the office, and right in front of my eyes they opened the cardboard file that was urgently brought up from the archives at my request. The photograph in the file, I noted right away, was the same photograph that has sat next to my dad's bed now for thirty-six years. Here is the list of the courses he signed up for, the secretary pointed out, and here is his tuition receipt.

. . .

We would find my grandfather standing in front of the refrigerator's icebox, his head stuck inside the cold. He accidentally put some cheese in there, once, and was scared to thaw it out, because who knows what it would taste like after so many days frozen solid. That was just the beginning. A few days after we received the notification of my uncle's death, two soldiers brought my grandfather the watch in an envelope. One of them said to him, I knew your son back in basic training. Which is what they told every bereaved father. In order to console him. It was the holiday of Sukkot, 1973. We went to the hotel courtyard and saw that a *sukkah* had been set up without branches covering the roof and with a table inside. The branches had been thrown to the ground. And in the *sukkah* decorations and photos were hanging, photos of his son (my uncle), and also photos no one in my family had ever seen before, photos of relatives and townspeople in Poland. And in his sleep—again and again he would fall asleep across from us in the living room of his apartment in the hotel—he would call out to them. And the rain fell on all the decorations and photographs in black and white he received from Yad Vashem and then enlarged and enlarged again, or that arrived with the handful of survivors buried inside the books they managed to take with them, or that photograph they took when in my grandfather's sake they dressed up and stood together and concentrated and stared right at me.

And the hotel was silent, most days. Only then did its downfall begin, since no one could worry about the guests anymore, nor did anyone collect any money from them, and so whoever registered for a night or for the High Holidays in October 1973 stayed for two or three months and sometimes even years, and there's one tenant who's about ninety years old, named Shimon, who resides there to this day, in a sort of side wing that became unsuitable for guests, in a corridor, and he sleeps on a children's bed that he dragged in from the street and cooks his meals for himself on a kerosene burner, and shuts himself up behind the wing's steel gate, which he himself welded in the middle of the night in order to close his territory off from whoever might want to remove him, and places ornate teakettles on his bed, because someone told him that according to Ottoman law this is enough, a bed and teakettles, in order to ensure legal possession of prop-

erty. But, after all, no one paid attention to him, no one ever considered removing him. He was put up in the hotel for the High Holidays and after Sukkot considered returning (to where?), but then the war broke out and what happened happened and he stayed, he couldn't abandon my grandfather and grandmother, leave them all alone there. And suddenly they didn't change his sheets anymore, and didn't serve him breakfast, and the bottles of water my grandmother Aliza would carbonate for the guests disappeared, because my grandmother forgot all about the hotel, and immersed herself in her Arabic studies. *Shu ismak? Min ha'da?* The sea burrowed under the limestone. I was informed of all this only years later, like the story about how my grandmother, in those days, started walking around Netanya with billions of the German Marks her father, Shlomo Goldring, "The Old Man," had brought from the city of Schmölln, Germany, in his overcoat, after which she'd unstitched them from the lining and distributed said billions to Netanya's poor, who quickly discovered that the bills were entirely worthless, and to this day it's possible to buy them in the stamp and currency store on Herzl Street. They keep those bills in crates, they'll never run out of them. She would stand in the kitchen facing the oven and would speak to everyone who entered the kitchen via that cold oven. Until October '73, animals disgusted her, especially cats. I'm allergic to them, she said, I see a cat and swell up. And then, after the Yom Kippur War, we suddenly found her with cats, three or four of them. And when we asked, Grandma, what is it with these cats all of a sudden, she looked at us, scrunched up her face, and said: And what if I'm a cat as well? It was many years before I was informed of all this, they spared me from the years of the hotel's decline, and I never saw with my own eyes my grandfather in torn clothes, the ashes of a spring-loaded ashtray heaped upon his scalp, I only heard about it from those who were there, perhaps twenty years later. But one day in October 1973, a photograph of my dad's brother appeared next to my dad's bed, the uncle who carried me on his shoulders had transformed into a photograph and never emerged from it again, and after some time, in December, my brother was born and they named the red-haired baby after the deceased. I know that inside me, in a hidden place, there remains, intact, the moment in which I came to know that my uncle fell in battle; certainly it was a shock I was unable to bear at the time. But that decisive moment is buried below the words on these pages, and even if I could retrieve it, disinter it and bring it to light—I wouldn't. That same winter, the beginning of 1974, my grandfather would often go down to the sea, a plastic hoe in his hand, and I would cover his feet in the cold sand, and he would cover the palms of my hands. Goldfish rose from the sea and were cut down by the tops of the waves. No, there weren't fish, it was just the light of the sunset. We went and tossed our sandwiches to the sunset, made crumbs out of the bread. The waves grabbed the crumbs even before they landed, while they were still in the air, and sometimes right out of our hands. My grandfather didn't know how to swim and I was a child, therefore we plodded along in the shallow water like two turtles. And he would go into the edge of the freezing water next to the lifeguard stand, or lay down in the wet sand and stick an ear into it, like he was listening to the earth, or stare at the locked lifeguard stand and at the black flag flapping in the wind and pointing in the direction of the city. Fish cages, he mumbled apropos of nothing. When my parents found out that he had again taken me to the sea in the cold without their knowledge, they would hurry to the beach down the stairs across from Independence Square and sometimes in their haste would come to us straight down the limestone hillside. But I was already asleep, packed up snugly in the wooden chest that my father and grandfather built for me when I was born, with wheels on the side and a bar for pulling, bottles filled with warm water to my right and to my left.

. . .

The lifeguard at the beach in Netanya said to us: I dream four dreams.

First Dream:
They sentence me to four months in prison. A child drowned.

I know who the child is. What's weird is there's another person being accused too. A childhood friend. I haven't seen him or thought about him since school. He flees and doesn't go to jail. On the way he throws his bag away. He has an old phone in the bag. I look for a phone jack and connect the phone. The lifeguard stand has plenty of phone jacks, it's like a switchboard of sorts. I consider calling his parents to tell them that he fled. I search for "father" in his address book, and I find it too, "father" is actually written there, but there's no number next to the word. All the names have numbers except for father. I go over all his numbers, and I see my number there as well. But it's not my name next to it. It's not my name.

Second Dream:
There's an elevator over the sea. Not an elevator in a straight shaft, but a sort of tangle of tracks. Like a giant ball of wool, but there are large spaces between the bundled-up strands. It's not a dense ball. There's a car that travels on the tracks. Like a roller coaster, but with multiple tracks, and they're more complex. And there are signs with the names of the stations, and I see the Netanya station in the distance. But I know there's no reason to get off, because afterward I'll just have to get back on the train again. I understand that it's impossible to leave these tracks, all you can hope for is to get off for a bit and then get back on again. Now I think that perhaps I could have jumped from the train to the sea and escaped after all. But in my dream this didn't occur to me, and I didn't know what to do. Anyway, in the dream the car got stuck. It always happens like that. Once, when I was a boy, the Ferris wheel got stuck when I was all the way at the top. I looked down and didn't see my grandfather, who had taken me to the amusement park. And then I recalled that he too had decided to get on the Ferris wheel after all, at the last minute. That is, he must have been in the next car. I try to see him there, but I can't.

Third Dream:
A fish swims up. Gray, large. But he also has some gold spots on him. He stops opposite me and tries to say something to me, but there's a sort of thick glass between us. I tell him to write to me on the glass, like in winter, when the frost covers the bus windows, and you can write in it with your finger.

Fourth Dream:
I arrive here at the beach like I do every morning (except for Friday) at five, before most of the bathers, in order to run a bit and wash up before the start of my shift. I say to myself in the dream, this is a wonderful thing, the sea. Everyday a different sea. Thank God this is my job. I go up to the stand to change my clothes, and as I open the door and turn on the light I see my mother sitting in the chair and looking out at the sea. I know that something horrible has happened, otherwise she wouldn't have come at a time like this all the way from Kalkilya. I stand next to the door with my hand on the switch, and she stares at the sea. I work up the courage to ask her, Mother, what happened? And it's strange, I think now, that in the dream I address her in Hebrew. And she, who also answers me in Hebrew, says, "Look for yourself." And I go and stand behind her and see that the sea has dried out. That everything you can see from here to the horizon is desert, sand dunes. I see a camel walking in the sea. And I hear the flag on the roof rapping in the wind. Tak, tak, tak. Tak, tak, tak! **Tak, tak, tak!**

. . .

When we returned from the poet Uri Zvi Grinberg's funeral, my grandfather asked me, do you remember the lifeguard on the beach? I knew his mother. She lived in Netanya once. Before there was an Israel. I was very friendly with her. A beautiful, refined woman. Do you remember his dream? I thought of his dream just now, and it reminded me of a dream of my own. I dreamed once that I was standing in line at some law court, and I saw there, in another line, the poet Leah Goldberg. I asked her, is everything okay, Ms. Goldberg? You were a guest of ours once in the hotel. I'm the son-in-law of Shlomo Goldring. And she answered me: I was never in your hotel. And I was never in Netanya. And I haven't heard of Mr. Goldring. But I know who you've got me mixed up with."

. . .

When they dug the foundations for the Park Hotel, a tall, modern place that was erected on the shore at the end of Bialik Street in Netanya, the diggers found a giant animal's skeleton at the edge of a limestone cliff looking out onto the sea. I remember the picture on the front page of *This Week in Netanya*, which my mother cut out and hung over my bed for me. It was impossible to mistake the giant tusks, much larger than those of today's elephant. I stood there next to my grandfather and my father, and I remember my grandfather was holding, absentmindedly, both of our hands. A burning cigarette was sticking out of his mouth. My father was then about the age I am now, thirty-nine, while I was thirteen years old. From a distance I noticed the astronomy teacher, who had come with students. He heard about the discovery on the radio and quickly went from house to house to gather up the students. He didn't find me, but his heart told him that this was because I was already there. The teacher waved hello to us and then with his chin pointed toward the massive skeleton that had sort of half emerged from the limestone, and next to it the yellow blade of a bulldozer, raised a bit in the air, teeth exposed. My grandfather took a couple steps forward, bent over the animal's large ribs, and slid his hand along them, wreathed in smoke, as though he were stroking soft fur, his gray brimmed hat tilting a bit, almost falling onto the bones.

The Park Hotel stands where that skeleton was found, though it went up in flames a few years after it was built. The hotel was renovated and then, many years later, in 2002, the Passover terrorist attack took place there, in which thirty people were murdered and more than a hundred were injured. Our astronomy class graduation ceremony was held on the roof of this hotel. That was in 1985, and by that time the roof of *our* family's hotel, Hotel Tel Aviv, had already collapsed like a sheet of paper into the top floor. The Park Hotel had reached new heights and our hotel had fallen apart. Each and every one of us brought his telescope, and that night they were pointed toward the four large moons of Jupiter and toward Saturn as well. The astronomy teacher went from eyepiece to eyepiece, and each time the rings of Saturn were revealed to him a bit differently, he said, as if it wasn't one planet and one set of rings out there, but rather fifteen Saturns and fifteen sets of rings and fifteen bands of shadow. In a drop of seawater, he said, it's sometimes possible to find more bacteria than there are people on planet Earth. The distances contained in the drop, for them, are no less great, he said, than the distance for us between Earth and Saturn's outermost rings. Traveling the distance from the outer to the inner ring at a sprint is a task that would do us in, if we could ever even reach the starting point, the outer ring. Imagine yourselves jumping from frozen rock to frozen rock in darkness, like children crossing a stream, and then, finally, reaching the inner border of the rings—that is, the inner edge of the innermost ring—and before you looms the chasm that extends down to Saturn itself. All you have to do is reach your hands out to your sides and jump, and Saturn's gravity will pull you inward, but you hesitate and stay put, watching the distant planet day after day, revolving slowly with its rings, which are nothing but bits of stone and ice. The bacteria look from one edge of the water drop to the other and think about infinity and what lies beyond it—that is, beyond the water drop's wall—just like us. The drop is clear and transparent and they don't understand how it can be that they see it at all, how it can exist both in their consciousness and out there, as it were. They assume that it exists independently and that they are a foreign element inside it. But they and the drop are one thing—this we know, but are unable to tell them. Drinking half a glass of water, said the astronomy teacher, before drinking half a glass of water, is to drink worlds upon worlds. A single bacterium can multiply in one day to a number of individuals greater than the number of human beings that have ever lived, and this knowledge always bewilders me and fills me with joy, he said. This is the power of life, he said, nothing can destroy it. The hand holding the glass of water can't help but shake. The gap between the smallest world and our world and the gap between the biggest world and our world is vast, but nevertheless we see each one of them through polished lenses. Most of us can barely converse with our fellow human beings and explain our troubles to them, can barely manage to explain even to our spouses what troubles us, and so it's no wonder that we can't say a thing to the great and the small, to galaxies and colonies of bacteria, despite wanting to—as we do, don't we?—despite wanting to speak with star colonies and microscopic colonies both. I want to translate from above to below, the astronomy teacher said, to find the word that can be heard in the stars and whisper it straight into the microscope, the word that will be understood both above and below and of course, the teacher said and cleaned the eye piece of my telescope a bit with a velvet handkerchief, I will understand it as well. It's reasonable to assume that the stars don't know anything about the millions of bacteria in a drop of water, and the bacteria apparently haven't heard a thing about galaxies. Actually, who knows. Perhaps it's only we who can serve as a go-between, translate from macro language to micro language, the teacher said, but up until now we've failed in this. I love bacteria deeply, he said, they maintain life on this planet, they purify the water and balance the level of oxygen in the atmosphere and help the plants to grow and the animals to digest their food. They're cast out over everywhere like a vast net. They are our forefathers. There is no limit to their wisdom. The stars above and the bacteria below, he said, these are the proper company for a decent man. Who knows if they don't control us and our lives and our thoughts through a hidden, ingenious system. Perhaps we are the city and they are the inhabitants, he said and fell silent. We settled into our sandwiches.

On the bench on Smuts it appeared to me that I could see Saturn and that I noticed its rings out of the corner of my eye, even though this was without doubt an illusion. Without a lens before us, how weak is our vision. Most of the universe is unseen. Even the seen is only just the outside of a door. People passed me by on the boulevard in the middle of the night and searched for relief from the heat. Two by two or in groups they walked its width and length, arm in arm or at a small distance from each other. On the boulevard's benches sat or lay neighbors and acquaintances. The gates of the synagogue were open (this was a few days before Tisha Ba'av, 2009) and there were those who went inside and stood close to the Ark or just grabbed a little coolness by the cantor's air conditioner, dragging fingers and nails along the pages and letters. On the bench opposite me lay a man I didn't know. With the tips of his fingers he waved hello to me. I waved back to him with the tips of my fingers.

...

I write these things as if I know the people involved, including myself, but this isn't correct. I don't know myself and I don't remember myself. Without photos even the little I appear to remember would vanish, for the most part. I can't traverse the distance to my grandfather or even to myself, and that's the truth. I write and write, observe and dig, report on what happened, and appear to get closer to myself and those people, the living and the dead. I'm not fabricating my childhood entirely, but I don't remember who I was at all. I look at childhood pictures and I don't remember that boy. Were they to tell me that he isn't me but instead, say, a cousin, I'd believe it. How similar we were, all the kids. I know my child-self no more and no less than I know the readers of this book. Then again, it could be that my child-self is me, and that what appears as distance is actually absolute proximity. Could be. I write this and am immediately struck with a headache. I prefer the prehistoric times described in science books, since they're more concrete for me than my memories of the seventies. This proximate time that is my time, the time of my life, I cannot see. I need to skip around, I need a series of skips, in order to get to my past. *I am that skipping*, and the skipping doesn't stop. The day will come when I'll read these lines in amazement and not remember that I wrote them, neither them nor this sentence itself. Everything is only remnants: stories blurry as the ruins of a hotel stuck in the middle of Netanya. *I must travel to the hotel*, I said to myself that same night on the bench on Smuts in Tel Aviv, I must travel to the Hotel Tel Aviv and be a guest there for one night and then everything will rise to the surface. The place will bring everything back. Get up, get in the car, and travel immediately to the hotel in Netanya, I said to myself, and didn't move from the bench. I saw myself hit the bell on the reception desk, behind which my grandmother used to sit, looking forward to being taken to my room, but the sound of the bell intensified and echoed until the reception desk, the wall of the hotel, the roof, everything cracked in loud silence and crumbled to dust. Were I to keep to memories I could support by way of reliable documentation, this manuscript would be able to fit into a box of matches. For me, all of childhood is maybe ten fragmented sentences, maybe twenty pictures from memory, not much more than this. Everything is forgotten or will be forgotten. In forty years of life there are about fifteen thousand sunrises. You remember maybe three, maybe one, and maybe you don't truly remember even that. I certainly saw many clouds then, I certainly dunked my head in the foam of the waves, I certainly swam down deep until they noticed me from shore and screamed to have me saved. I certainly saw the central bus station in the light of dawn and all the drivers holding coffee in disposable cups and sitting down with heavy groans. But what remains of them? What remains is crushed liked the potatoes that turned to embers in the campfire. The words always arrive late, too late, and are only useful for others, if at all. You pretend that you can make mashed potatoes from those potatoes, but these mashed potatoes are nothing but a pile of cold ash that you bend over and sink your teeth and eyes into.

...

In their book *The Life and Death of Planet Earth*, Ward and Brownlee describe what's expected to happen on our planet in the distant future, according to the current findings of astrobiological science. Following the man-made warming, fossil fuels will run out, and the ice age, from which we were removed only twelve thousand years ago, will return to our world. The terrible ice. After that will come the heat, the heat of the expanding sun, whose future is to swallow all of planet Earth. On the far side of this book, as on the far side of all books, stands no book, a cloud of dust, a thick layer of frost. I imagine the music collection I've accumulated over the years in the face of the expanding sun or in the frigid arms of the extreme cold. The day will arrive when all music will freeze and disappear. There are those who believe in the existence of music in another dimension, an eternal one, but music itself teaches us to confront the extinction awaiting us and it, since by being itself music becomes extinct again and again. Each note appears at the same time it becomes extinct. Its appearance is also its disappearance. When I understood this I breathed easy. Every moment of existence is also a moment of nonexistence. Thus, music is possible, thus it is possible to live. Music sings an elegy to itself, the pianist Brad Mehldau wrote. I also sing an elegy to myself, and in this regard I am no different than any person or any musical composition. And like music, I strive to sing this elegy joyfully. When the officers of the fallen arrived at the hotel, my grandfather was in the carpentry shed that he built for himself in the hotel's courtyard, next to the shriveled-up orange tree that produced dry and sour fruit, from which my grandfather would squeeze juice for us. He sawed boards and whistled cantorial tunes, as was his habit. I'll never know what happened that day, but the saw remained stuck in the board and the glue that stood in its wooden box congealed and the nails that were attached to a magnet remained attached. Neither my grandfather nor my father ever entered the carpentry shed again. I would go inside again and again and look at the saw that had sawed through a third of the way, at the magnetized nails stuck to the metal block, at the glue that became a yellowish mass with a dead fly trapped inside, at the strips of Formica glued to the table, at the vise tightened around two boards that were intended for a closet door. The vise couldn't be loosened. My father would start out turning it forcefully and then my grandfather would add another rotation, additional tightening. I could sense the pressure of the metal on the wood. I sensed it as if it were fastened around my temples. I saw the giant nails attached to the black magnet, whose shape was that of a massive horse's hoof, and the glue that no force in the world could ever remove from its box. After the death of my grandfather, the carpentry shed was destroyed and the courtyard of the hotel was covered in asphalt and turned into a parking lot, where you can still park today, and indeed I parked there myself when I went to take some pictures of the place. I drove on past and stopped. In the place of the orange tree stood the parking attendant's booth, and in my rearview mirror I saw him dig a yellowed fingernail into a grapefruit and peel it.

During one of my last visits with my grandfather, after he moved from the hotel to an old folks' home, I opened a low cabinet at his request in order to remove some medicine at the bottom. The cabinet was very deep, and I had to lay flat on the floor and reach my hand inside and feel around. It was impossible to see anything inside. My grandfather, from his bed, said, "Wait a moment, I'll give you some light," and from under his pillow he removed a large flashlight. In the flickering yellow glare I noticed, from my position, close to the floor, next to the door of the low cabinet, my cheek up against the floor, my teeth nearly touching the tiling, next to the many medications piled up there, medication for diabetes but also cartons of a certain cigarette that hadn't been produced for twenty years now, a box of glue, and the water level that's now hung in my room as a mezuzah, as well as a hammer he made himself and a few giant nails. He'd brought the tools to the old folks' home when he moved, and after his death the director of the old folks home said to me: Certainly, he fixed many things for us too. I raised my eyes and looked from below at my grandfather sitting on the bed, still pointing the beam of the flashlight at the low cabinet even though I had already removed his medications. At the edge of the room was a chair inside a chair inside a chair. He was about ninety years old already. Only then did I notice, from my place on the floor, for the first time after years of visits, that the rusty vise was fastened around the leg of the bed next to the wall and holding it to the rest of the bed, fastened around the short leg with such immense pressure that it gave me the chills—to the point that the wood was cracked and splintering down its entire length.

. . .

They had a class on immortality at the old folks' home. According to the principles of Daoism. They brought in an expert of sorts, named Nir. He was kind of skinny, always dressed in loose linen clothes, curly-haired, a devout vegan, germinating and eating all day long. Anyone who eats non-sprouted food, he said to me once, is either a fool or is lost. No: only sprouted. Since I had a warm cheese muffin in my bag, I kept quiet. He would write Chinese symbols in chalk on a board and give the residents golden pills he himself concocted. He was always germinating things and passing them out to everyone. He would tell them to inhale and hold the air and not exhale. He would tell them not to eat certain things. Would suddenly embrace Swiss chard. Leaves and stems. And practicing Tai Chi and Chi Gong. Some of the residents were old and stooped, one hundred years of age, ninety years of age. You will never die, he told them. And me, too, he said, I will never die either. This class will never end, he said. And in fact, other than my grandfather, who died in the meantime, all those old people are still alive. The teacher is still alive, too.

. . .

At the age of fourteen on my desk at school I drew in pencil the entire solar system and added to it space ships and formulas and creatures. Were this desk still in my possession I would attach it to this book as evidence. But the desk, or the drawing on it anyway, no longer exists, for that very day, as punishment, the teacher commanded me to erase the desk, that is, the solar system. I looked at the symbol π and for a moment said to myself, there is a fixed ratio between me and anything that can be indicated by a sign. This entire book is that sign. The same sensation pulsed in me as it pulsed in me that night on the bench and as it pulses in me while writing these lines as well. I don't know what the thing is, the thing to which I'm connected by a fixed ratio, but if I'm the radius, then I have a circle, without a doubt. With the large eraser I was given specifically for the serving of my sentence, I erased all the circles and the formulas, I erased everything, and the classroom filled up with the signs of erasure, little bits of white rubber. But I wasn't satisfied with the eraser and brought a bucket of water and soap and scoured the desks well, and then I squeegeed away the water filled with rubber bits, and I squashed the filthy dough into a ball that I threw into the garbage. Before the punishment of erasure was inflicted upon me, my desk and the solar system I drew on it, along with an interstellar angel, with the help of elliptical rulers and compasses, was presented as an object of ridicule to the entire class. It was put on display as incriminating evidence: lifted up and set onto the teacher's desk, which I scoured with hot water as well, even though it was already spotless. My desk was put on display, and I myself was forced to sit without a desk for the rest of the day. I continued to sit like this, without a desk, even after everyone went home. Afterward, I got up and started erasing, and when my parents came to get me they found me in the corner of a scoured classroom. All the desks were clean as new, aside from my desk, which was still sitting on the teacher's desk with the solar system on it. I'd erased all the desks save mine. I was ordered to erase my desk, but I erased all the other desks, and I left my desk as it was. The classroom had never been so clean, the desks and the floor that I cleaned along the way were fragrant and sparkling, but on the teacher's clean desk lay my desk. I knew I wouldn't be able to leave the room without erasing my desk as well, but I couldn't do it myself, and therefore

I gave the damp eraser to my mother and left. This teacher at the school, which was a junior high in a yeshiva for high school students, expressed a blanket rejection of the "laws of nature" that I learned in astronomy class. He wasn't ready to take any chances with the idiotic pull of gravity, much less with that bad joke, evolution. That's all we need, said the teacher who imposed the punishment of erasure on me and even offered praise the next day for the thorough erasing I'd performed, that's all we need, for the entire class to start floating among the stars. Don't talk to me about light years, I can barely make it through a tax year, he said. He remembered the incident well, and on the day of my grandfather's funeral it amused him just as much as it had back then. I shook his hand warmly and turned to leave the cemetery. Near the entrance, I turned to look back and saw how despite the twenty years that had passed, he hadn't aged at all, even looked young, almost a teenager, and saw how he bent over, entirely red, in order to place a stone on the new pile of dirt, as is customary. I went over to the faucets to wash my hands, as I had done then, at school, when I left the class with my father. Then we noticed that my mother wasn't with us in the courtyard. We turned our heads. Looking through the window from outside, we saw her, sitting in the classroom on a low chair, studying the solar system.

. . .

There was a student in my class who was a comet. At night, his parents said at his funeral, he would run up Bialik Street to the corner of King David Street, throw himself forcefully into the air, and glide over the sea, then escape from gravity, and after a few rounds would pick up speed and shoot toward the solar wind. Clearly he kept his distance from the sun itself. From there his route was plotted in a regular, elliptical way. Sometimes one nocturnal orbit sufficed, and he returned home in the morning, tired and disheveled, grabbed a little cereal and milk, and rode his bike to school, barely awake. He would fall asleep in class, even in astronomy class. The rest of us students didn't suspect a thing, and we mistakenly thought that the ice sometimes stuck in his hair was dandruff, and so we nicknamed him "The Carp" on account of how scaly he seemed. The carp didn't tell anyone about his life as a comet. Because what could he say? We wouldn't have believed anything so outlandish.

The carp came to a nasty end. One day he didn't show up at school, and his parents sent word that he had a cold. A few days later the truth came out—the boy had crashed, he and his tail, into one of Jupiter's moons. It's hard to describe a comet's terror at the moment it understands that it's doomed to crash into a planet, let alone a settled planet, his mother told me, for I was the only student in the whole class who came to visit them during their seven days of mourning. For one long night or hundreds of years they race from the far periphery to the center in hopes that the day will finally come when they'll return to their point of origin on the far side of the ellipse they've sketched all their lives. Like a truck loaded with rocks and ice that sets out in the morning to make its rounds and finds when it returns to base that in the spot where there was always an open parking space there is now an unmovable, armored wall. And the driver wants to honk but there's no horn, and he wants to brake but there are no brakes, and he wants to scream but it's impossible to scream. And people accuse him of crashing into the wall intentionally, and flee from him in terror, and most everyone hates him too, and they kick his tires, no one understands, from his perspective *they* crashed into *him*, it was they who wanted to prevent his return. We close our eyes when he falls on us, as it were, his mother said, but for him—there are no eyes to close. The carp's mother went to the porch and returned with her son's bicycle and gave it to me as a gift, lock and all. I asked her if they weren't afraid, she and her son, that the day would come when he would crash into planet Earth, and maybe even into their home in the center of Netanya. His mother looked at me sadly and said, if he had thought there was a great chance that this would happen, her son would never have headed out toward what is for us black empty space, but which was for him his only home.

. . .

On one of the memorial days for fallen soldiers my uncle came to give a talk at our school. But since naturally he could no longer speak, he carried a doll, a sort of marionette the army had supplied him with. It was a rainy day and the doll spoke in the rain.

For years nothing happens, and then, as in the Cambrian explosion approximately half a billion years ago, everything flows, abounds, multiplies. I speak of course about writing as well. This abundance is no better or worse than stagnating or drying up. But something changes in the atmosphere, there's more oxygen, for example, and while this oxygen surely kills multiple species inside you, to other species it gives life. And sometimes you yourself are born out of it. And sometimes you aren't. Something dies out and something new arises. And there's no knowing if the new is better than the old. But there's certainly change. Suddenly you find yourself on a stool, holding a notebook. Life on Earth was not, it appears, created in the pastoral pool Darwin imagined, nor in the green Garden of Eden we read about in our childhood, but rather in a boiling world, in an atmosphere abundant in carbon dioxide, perhaps with volcanic activity on the ocean floor, with high pressure and murky water and little light. For there, at that great depth, was protection from the frequent comet and meteor strikes and from the radiation coming from the sun. But life was created, and soon began making itself extinct by its own hand. Jared Diamond, in his book, *Guns, Germs, and Steel*, describes how in 1835 the Maori from New Zealand slaughtered the inhabitants of the nearby island Chatham, the Moriori. They slaughtered them "according to our customs," as they put it, since they wanted to enslave the Moriori, but their neighbors tended to resist that sort of treatment. The Moriori, who had a tradition of pacifism, did not fight the invaders, but offered a solution of peace. Therefore they were overwhelmed and annihilated. This story weighs heavily on the heart and the soul, as do hundreds of similar stories. You don't know a single Moriori but it's nevertheless your story, and every person's story. More than this, the slaughtering Maori and the slaughtered Moriori were a single people, researchers say, which split up onto two islands a thousand years earlier, and thanks to the different causal conditions on the two islands evolved in different ways. The Maori thought they were slaughtering a distant, inferior, foreign tribe, when they were actually slaughtering their kinsmen. And isn't this always, always the story. It's our story too. The Syrian soldier in the tank who killed my uncle was our distant relative, and under different circumstances we could have sat at a table and broken bread together. In my uncle's tank crew there was a young man whose parents came to Israel from Khaleb, Syria a few years earlier, only for their son to be sent to fight against other Syrians. There's something especially depressing in all these stories of annihilation when one factors in the understanding of just how rare life is, and the fact that every murder is always a murder within the family, that is patricide or infanticide or unclicide or brother-in-lawcide or cousincide. Simply because your distant cousin speaks a different language, you enslave him; simply because the color of your distant cousin's skin is different, you rape her cruelly and cut off her head with your axe. The one thing capable of easing the distress caused by this knowledge, at least a little bit, not to mention the distress caused by the evil operating day after day and moment after moment upon helpless people, plants, and animals, is the feeling of wonder in the face of life's potency, which, in the depths of the oceans, in the opening of a volcano covered in salt water, whose color was apparently purple, creates new forms, stubbornly and perpetually. Life bursting forth wherever it can, even out of the tiniest crack. Over the course of two billion years, this microscopic life will become Maoris and Morioris, and the Maori will slaughter the Moriori according to their customs. The wonder and the horror are two names for the same process, and except on rare occasions most Israeli literature does its best to ignore this. Instead of presenting us with the big picture or at least hinting at it, our literature time and again presents a small picture, a fraudulent picture. The small picture is a picture of absolute despair or idiotic happiness, and from this perspective there's no difference between the gloomy kitsch of the theater of the absurd and the sweet kitsch of Hollywood. Black kitsch and pink kitsch, same thing. The pessimism and the optimism that most literature and art sell to their audience are drugs, just as addictive and just as deadly as the real thing, and so people pass through life moving from joy to depression and back again, and again. The book *Rare Earth*, without which I now understand that this book, which I will call *Netanya*, would not have been written, speculates that microorganisms, such as bacteria, can travel from planet to planet, that is, hitch rides inside meteors, and, more, transport themselves along with the distant migrations of those birds made of cold rock, those peacocks whose tails are ice, that is, comets. A bacterium can survive a journey through space trapped in ice. It races through vast fields of darkness, trapped in ice or rock and waits. Who knows if a few bacteria that arrived on Earth with Martian meteors weren't our ancient grandmother. But where did she come from before Mars, that's a good question, which will have to be answered in due time. A rock like that, which falls on someone's head or wipes out an entire city or continent, is sometimes, simultaneously, the beginning of life. In a drop of water, as I noted, there can be as many bacteria as there are people on Earth; that is, it's enough for one drop of water to fall on an uninhabited planet for it to be considered densely populated. Each and every year, now as well, a few hundred kilograms of matter from space falls on Earth. This matter can simultaneously destroy and fertilize, and it may be that some of the epidemics that have visited humanity over its history came from these rocks. For this reason as well as all the others, life on Earth is a constant process of destruction and renewal, certainly not one of steady construction. Sometimes a plague comes down and then everything ceases almost entirely. In any case, life on Earth could not have been created solely from local materials. That much is certain, just as the pyramids of Egypt and the grand Ancient Egyptian culture in its entirety could not have existed without food imported to Egypt from the Fertile Crescent, as Diamond writes in *Guns, Germs, and Steel.* Our hotel in Netanya was also built from Egyptian stone, as I've already noted. Each pyramid is Egyptian only on the surface; actually, the pyramids are a product of Mesopotamian culture no less than Egyptian. Without Mesopotamian wheat, the Egyptian Sphinx would not have been built—this is a fact. More than psychoanalysis and the whole of literary theory, there, on the bench, these facts and others like them clarified my life and what could be called my literary output. I, too, had my Mesopotamia; I, too, was struck by asteroids in the head and in the stomach: Some were small asteroids that only scratched my face, and some were enormous asteroids that struck my stomach forcefully or entered my head and never left, throbbing in there like a molten pit. At the center of the Earth there's a pit as well, a core, a sort of inner sun, and it creates Earth's magnetic field. Without this core, a sort of ancient aunt who sits there knitting a warm thick sweater twenty-four hours a day, the Earth's protective magnetic field would not exist—that is, *we* would not exist. Our aunt wraps us up in the magnetic blanket necessary for our existence, but we don't visit our aunt because it's impossible to get down deep enough to see her. This aunt is also one of the deeper explanations for the existence of literature, only literature ignores her, isn't interested in her, just as most writers don't visit their aunts, instead sitting in cafés and debasing their hours with gossip, which is the custom in the literary world. This core that I'm calling our aunt can be found in a fugue by Bach as well as in these lines. In a fugue by Bach there is an inner core and it's possible to hear it in every note just as it's possible to hear the aunt in every aunt wandering around the surface of the Earth and doing their holiday shopping. We are all the aunt, this is what I'm arguing actually, this is my metaphor. The atmosphere, the land, and the oceans, they are a single, integrated process. Plankton dies, sinks, and transforms into rock, and the rock melts and bursts out of a volcano, now that's what I'd call sleight of hand. The atmosphere maintains life and life maintains the atmosphere, or, in the case of modern humanity, destroys and poisons it. But "human" and "atmosphere" are one organism, one thing, and we don't understand this. We're like an idiotic turtle that gnaws on his own shell because it seems to him that the shell isn't part of his body, or an idiotic fish that dries up the sea in which he lives because in his opinion the sea is separate from him. The fish says, "I am not made of sea, and therefore I will dry up the ocean." The turtle says, "What do I have to do with this shell?" And thus they bring upon themselves their end. Idiocy of this sort is humanity's daily routine, and I, too, act idiotically, for example every time I get into my car, and every time I publish a book, including this book, which in the name of justice should be tossed into the recycling bin immediately upon being read and perhaps even before that, I thought on the bench, and looked at my car, parked nearby, covered with bits of dew. A '98 model. A wrinkled old can. From the previous century. We imagine that the atmosphere is a thin, distant layer of air that surrounds the earth, but the atmosphere is located in our lungs, here, in our actual mouths, between our teeth.

One of the things that endangered the beginning of life on the young Earth was the impact of the big rocks, the meteors and the comets. But the impact of the big rocks was apparently also what enabled life, and certainly our lives, because the same rocks carried ice that melted and became water that became steam that returned and condensed, becoming lakes and seas and oceans. And perhaps the meteors and the comets even carried those tiny bits of life that we call bacteria and which were our forefathers. The comets vaporized the water with their impact but brought fresh water in their tails. When I read this I knew that I was reading a description of myself, of my life. When my solar system (on the table) was destroyed, when I asked my mother to erase the solar system I had drawn, I had to draw another solar system immediately, and so I did. My uncle was killed in the war and this struck our entire family and it strikes us even today, though we don't feel it much anymore. But since the age of three and a half I've said no to war. It's clear that I could have said yes to war because of my uncle's death in battle, but I said no to war and I continue to say no to war, and have been doing so since the age of three and a half. At the age of three and a half I suddenly said to my mother: no to war, and everyone thought that I heard this on television or on the radio. At the age of three and a half I said no to war, and at the age of four I already knew how to read and write; my mother taught me and with this my education was actually completed, I should point out. My uncle's death was the comet that struck me at quite an early stage in my creation and was most devastating. It changed the tilt of my axis in relation to the sun and I am still tilted toward her at the same angle produced by the force of that impact, and these lines are irrefutable proof of this. My uncle was killed and I thought again and again that the fallen could have been my father. My angle is twenty-three degrees and not ninety degrees, though the angle of this book's readers is no doubt different. From your place on distant planets you look through high-powered binoculars or telescopes, seeing everything. It's entirely clear—and there's no need for psychologists in this case—that every word written here deals with that same meteor strike, which took place on October 9th, 1973. A meteor struck Netanya but no one paid attention except me. My grandfather came here and thus survived the Holocaust that fell upon his family about five or six years later, but the force of his arrival also gave birth to his son Shalom who was killed in the Golan Heights at the age of twenty-one during his pre-release vacation. He was the youngest son, his two older brothers remained, one of whom is my father. My grandfather entered his ice age in October 1973. My grandfather's ice age took the appearance of diabetes and heavy smoking. What is called the Pleistocene began two and half million years ago and lasted until just around 12,000 years ago. This was the last severe ice age, and my grandfather entered his Pleistocene then, which felt to him as if it lasted just as long as the other one, and only came to an end with his death. In relation to geological epochs, he lived in what could be called "the Little Ice Age," as do hundreds and thousands of bereaved parents and those suffering from post-traumatic stress disorder, whose numbers multiply here from day to day. Sometimes you go out to the street and every parked car has a disabled tag, each sidewalk lined with these bitter reminders. My grandfather would go out in a thick overcoat he inherited from the "Old Man," no matter how hot it was, an overcoat in which money had once been sewn until my grandmother scattered it before the eyes of all Netanya, and when he would pass before the Ark on the High Holidays he insisted on all the fans being turned off for fear that he would catch cold and die. Every year he would travel to the Golan Heights, for the memorial ceremony for soldiers of the 82nd regiment, and he would leave for it bundled up like a man embarking on a journey to the North Pole. During an ice age, a thick layer of ice on the oceans prevents reciprocity between the water and the atmosphere—this too is written in *Rare Earth*, a book I believe I might already have mentioned. It's not only cold during an ice age, but the basic composition of the atmosphere changes as well. And if that weren't enough, the ice-covered planet sends most of the sun's rays back to space, like a giant mirror, so the planet cools even more. It cools down even more because of the cold, the cold creates cold, and the cold creates cold, my grandfather said in Yiddish, which I didn't understand then, and today I understand well. The cold drags along additional cold, this is the doctrine of the ice age in its essence, and its power is a fitting compliment for both Earth and my grandfather, Zvi Burstein. But the end of an ice age can be the beginning of new life-forms, as occurred with the completion of the ice age that came to an end approximately five hundred and forty million years ago and enabled the Cambrian explosion and the profusion of trilobites of which I am a descendant, though there's no doubt that there was life before them, it's just that those forms of life didn't leave behind fossils because they lacked hard organs. This book was written by a trilobite and was edited by a trilobite, and the printers and publicist and the copy editor and translator are also trilobites. As are the readers. My grandfather was born in an ice age and he lived his whole life in it, but in 1973 the ice's grip tightened even more. There were brief thaws of course, but the nature of the epoch was clear. My grandfather was born in 1915, the time of the First World War; he was an adult during the time of the Second War World, during which almost his entire family was wiped out; and in the Yom Kippur War he lost his youngest son, Shalom. He also lost my grandmother, Aliza, daughter of the "Old Man," living another twenty years following her death. She died of pneumonia after one of her grandchildren breathed into a birthday balloon but didn't manage to inflate it, so she took the balloon from him and inflated it and thus inhaled straight into her lungs the air her grandson had blown into it, which turned out to be the air of pneumonia, which the child survived, but she did not. She inhaled the grandson's infected lungs straight into her elderly lungs, and within days got sick and died. In the old folks' home my grandfather saw many great-grandchildren, among them my son and daughter, while sitting on his bed, one of whose legs would fall apart every few months because of the air from the sea, at the edge of which the old folks' home stood. The sea is eating the bed, he would say. The ice covered him more and more but he handed out oranges and pieces of chocolate. There's no need to fear death, he said to me in Yiddish in his twilight days, you will always exist in the universe in some way, this is quite clear. You go up on stage and leave and return, existence lasts so many years that it's best to change roles from time to time. You don't want to portray Othello or Lear or Prospero half a billion years in a row, he laughed suddenly, and hugged me. He read Shakespeare in Yiddish translation. There is no role so good that you wouldn't want to switch from time to time. After fifty performances, after five hundred performances, you want a new role even if you're Henry the Fifth himself, and this death grants you. Therefore every actor needs to be grateful for death. Death casts us and knows when the time has arrived for each of us to switch roles, and every second someone's role needs changing, therefore death is not lacking for work, I heard a song like that once on the radio, he said. The best role is the role of the fool, he said to me, even though every role is a fool's role, there is no other role. Death takes Hamlet, that is Hamlet the fool, and Hamlet the fool needs to learn by heart the role of King Lear the fool, or else death takes Macbeth the fool and Macbeth transforms into Francisco the fool from *Hamlet* and he suddenly finds himself saying those four wonderful words, "Stand and unfold yourself," and he doesn't know what his lips are speaking. They exchange roles not only between plays but within the same play as well. Usually, one actor receives multiple roles after the casting is redone. Sometimes two roles and sometimes ten thousand roles. Today he is Agamemnon the fool, tomorrow he is King Lear the fool and Uncle Vanya the fool and the moon of a distant planet and an almond tree and a thrush and a black hole, which is the heart of a galaxy of a hundred thousand worlds. From the spirit of a day-old baby perhaps a star cluster is created, and from a pulsar, a white lily, I thought on the bench, as sweat flowed over me and trickled drop by drop to the wooden boards. "Stand and unfold yourself," I said out loud, I screamed at one or two in the morning from my place on the bench, without knowing why I was saying this or to whom, but I knew well that everything was in these words. I didn't know then whom I was addressing with the words "stand and unfold yourself," but today I know that I was speaking to myself. Our entire conversation on the theater was conducted in Yiddish, my grandfather and I. He lived in an ice age, according to his own definition, although in his old age, every few years, and in his final days as well, it seemed that he was freed from the ice, but at the price of the loss of memory and the final collapse of the body. I live, at least at the time of the writing of these lines, in an epoch of relative warmth. My grandfather absorbed the cold of his son's death for me as Jupiter absorbs into itself stray comets and meteorites. But planets change the tilt of their axes, and *Rare Earth* describes how because of changes like these in the angle of a planet's tilt, equatorial landmasses become poles, and poles become equatorial regions. The cold can heat up and the heat can cool down, and the play changes, the entire stage is dismantled and built once again. This is a fatal change, polar bears wake up one morning to a tropical climate, and reef fish freeze under massive icebergs with their mouths agape. In our lives the change can occur in a moment. The change in the tilt of planet's axis can occur over millions of years, whereas the change in a human life can occur overnight. In the blink of an eye. You go to sleep in Netanya's pleasant heat and wake up in the morning to white landscapes at fifty degrees below zero, and the sun will never set on you ever again.

. . .

He traveled to a cantorial concert at the Jerusalem Theater. This was perhaps in 1984. I know because he told me so when he came to pick me up from astronomy class. They reported it in the news, the cantor was run over by a cement mixer an hour before the concert, and so the concert was played on a record player. All sorts of Jewish comedy songs, Klezmer tunes, "Kol Nidre." But this isn't what I wanted to tell you, he said. We were walking together, and he stopped next to the corner of Herzl Street. When I left the concert, he said, I turned around suddenly, for no reason, and raised my head. And on the roof of the building, on the roof of the Jerusalem Theater, he told me, there was a tank. Right on the edge of the roof. I stood there in the big frozen plaza. And there was a tank on the roof. It's a large cement building. A terrible building, my grandfather said to me, everything they build in Jerusalem today is atrocious. And on the building, right next to the parapet, was a tank. In the corner. The corner of the roof. There was a tank on the roof of the theater. Next to the parapet. Someone put it up there.

. . .

For years, an ancient, prehistoric grandfather was spoken about in my family, but I hadn't supposed that the horns resembling the horns of a northern deer, which were hanging above the door to the den and were passed on through the family from generation to generation, were actually his—that is, his own horns. A simple DNA test that I did myself verified the rumor, which I learned after the fact had also been passed down, from mouth to mouth, through my family. "Certainly," my mother said, amazed at my amazement, "with us nothing gets thrown out. And while we're on the subject, there's also that tusk behind the refrigerator, why it's been sitting there for years . . . why not take it, take, take, c'mon take it, what am I going to do with it, take it . . ." That same day I climbed up a ladder and took the horns down from the wall. They were attached to a sort of rounded surface, like a stiff, horny yarmulke. I placed the yarmulke on my head. It fit like a glove; more than this, a powerful vacuum fastened it tightly to my scalp, and the more I tried to remove it the tighter it got. In the open closet, which was cold as a refrigerator and illuminated with a similar little light inside, the fur overcoat waited for me. Notes my grandfather had written were still inside it, and one or two of his father's banknotes were still sewn into the lining and rustled when I put my hands in its sleeves and my fingers were lost in its depths, on the other side of its elbow patches. In a side pocket was a scrap of paper, on which was a faded sketch of a prehistoric, hairy elephant. The smell of the cloak filled the house and we had to open the windows. We smashed them and the cold burst inside like it had been waiting for just this opportunity. My mother and aunt lit a fire. I wrapped myself in the cloak, and it covered my body down to the ankles. The sleeves dragged behind me like tails. I stood next to the front door barefoot and watched everyone sitting around the fire. They opened the door for me with a kick. I went out into the heavy snow.

. . .

I went to visit him at the old folks' home. He wasn't in his room, but in the small synagogue on the ground floor. Wearing a knitted cap, he raised his eyes from the Talmud. For a moment he didn't recognize me. And then he saw I wasn't wearing a yarmulke. He rose, tore out a page of the Talmud, folded it up with firm movements into a paper boat. With mouth tightly closed, he held it out for me, so that I'd place it on my head.

. . .

The grief over every fire he heard about, his fear of sudden conflagrations, immersing the tips of his cigarettes in cups of coffee and then removing them to verify that no ember remained, and his terror of large gas stations, rags soaked in kerosene, soaked thoroughly, and someone runs a comb through his hair or rubs it with coarse wool, and there's a spark, and it turns out that the hair was shampooed with kerosene in order to kill lice, and even the guy's sweater carries the scent of gasoline—everything is soaked in inflammable oil, everything in Israel is gasoline and combustible gases, a layer of oil floats over the Kinneret and someone goes in and puts out a cigarette in the ashtray sea. My grandfather would put a cigarette in his mouth and present me with the box of matches so that I'd light it for him. He had long matches that my father brought him as a gift from Switzerland, and they would light just from the slightest contact with the rough surface of their box. I would bring the match up to his cigarette and he would close his eyes and inhale, saying, "Put out the match, you're about to get burned."

. . .

Again they made us an effigy for the Lag B'Omer holiday bonfire. A mother of one of the kids worked at the wax museum in the Shalom Tower in Tel Aviv, and she took some materials lying around here and there, some fabric, some synthetic hair, some wax, some body paint, and made the enemy out of wax. We watched her progress, she could be seen from their balcony, she started with the head, of all things, at first she made it screaming, that is, speaking; afterward it became contemplative, like *The Thinker*, and then screaming again. In the meantime she made a raised fist that hovered next to the mouth. And one day a leg appeared, she took it whole from another figure, an amputee, the museum had made it two legs by mistake. She worked right up until Lag B'Omer, and while the children gathered up the final boards she was still working diligently on its eye makeup, she didn't know what color they should be, since she only had black and white pictures. And then she dressed it in a uniform she sewed over long nights like the nights she passed when she escaped to the Soviet Union, where she stayed during the war and met my grandmother from my mother's side, who didn't live in Netanya but in Ramleh instead. From her we learned that my grandmother had left a daughter in an orphanage, just temporarily, and when she came back two days later the girl was no longer there. She returned to the orphanage, this was in the center of the Soviet Union—she said "Siberia" but everything was "Siberia" then—and went from room to room, and there were children sitting in every room, small and thin and apparently weak but alive, they had a vegetable garden in the rear courtyard, and they worked there and grew fruits and vegetables for themselves, and at night they would sing songs from their distant homelands, since children from all across the Soviet empire had gathered there because of the advance of the Eastern Front. She heard different languages, Kazakh and Uzbek and Chechen and Bukhari and Georgian and Russian, and Yiddish of course, but she was scared to say a word in Yiddish, because she knew that if they heard her the Jewish children wouldn't let go. And she went from room to room there, and sometimes approached one of the girls and looked at her from up close, and thought perhaps this is her, perhaps she got thin while she was there, but it wasn't her, no. And no one knew where her girl had disappeared to, maybe she escaped in order to search for my grandmother, maybe, maybe, maybe. And in one of the rooms she saw two boys sitting and eating an onion, they were twins, and they carefully sliced the onion in two and divided it as she entered, my grandfather told the neighbor from the wax museum, and from the mumbling out of their mouths I knew they were Jews, she said, and I sat down between them, and I described for them the girl I'd left there two days earlier, I asked if they'd seen a girl resembling her, and the first said no, there hasn't been a new girl in the institution for three weeks now, and he knows since he's the monitor, and the other one looked at the monitor, that is, his brother, with contempt and said, nonsense, I saw a girl exactly like that, two days ago, room 16, I poured her soup, I'm the cook's helper aren't I, sure, she was here and ate soup with me. I don't know much more about my grandmother from my mother's side, but what I do know well is that my passion for baked goods, warm bread, rolls, fresh cakes, and pastry pies, and especially cheese muffins, I got from her, who after years of hunger in exile in Russia immigrated to Ramleh, and lived in "abandoned property" with her family, and worked in Ramleh in a bakery, and her daughters, my mother and her sister, helped her with the kneading and mainly with cleaning up the sticky dough that hardened on the stainless-steel surfaces. Thus my mother and her sister went through their childhood scraping dough, and the sole compensation was the warm bakery, the challahs and the breads, which they ate with no restrictions, kneaded and ate, baked and kneaded and pinched and sliced, and me too, just like them, I knead and bake, there's always bread in my oven. And sometimes I look at it, at the bread, and tremble.

At night we would hear the sewing machine plowing ahead in the silence of Bialik Street. And in the final days before Lag B'Omer the balcony's shutter was slammed shut and the neighbor from the wax museum closed the window and we heard nothing and saw nothing. But it was difficult to return to our games, we knew that something was going on there. Her son went to our school, though he was in a different grade. One day we cornered and interrogated him. He said, pale and forlorn, "She already did five, now she's doing the sixth." We let him go. He walked down the corridor, close to the wall, and once he was far away he stopped and slowly turned and looked at us. But we weren't there.

Right before someone was already about to light a match, she appeared, a rattling of a wheelbarrow announcing her arrival, her son running next to her. The effigy sat in a wax armchair made to look like a leather armchair, and was wearing a uniform of leather, and looking at an open wax book with thin wax pages, white as a candle. And someone said, "Look how small she made him. Why so small?" She gestured for her son to help her lift the dummy from the wheelbarrow and place it on top of the bonfire, on a crate tied to the top of the center pole. We wanted to applaud, but how could we? Everyone had hoped she wouldn't bring it, but we knew that after so many days of work this would be impossible. Only then did she order her son to go ahead and light the thing. "Burn it," she said quietly. "Give it some fire." But neither he nor any other child could approach it. "You worked so hard," said Mr. Kligler, the neighbor from Belgium, in French, and in his hand were a bunch of envelopes with the stamps cut off, which he had brought in order to burn along with the letters inside them. He would always bring a bunch of envelopes like that, the fire would consume the letters before the wood. They would rely on his letters for kindling, and he never disappointed.

My grandfather stood there the entire time, a warm, grilled potato from another fire in his hand. He couldn't identify the dummy, it didn't resemble anything. She used all sorts of leftovers from various world leaders and only years later did we understand her intention. Maybe I'm making it all up, but there was a dummy, there was a uniform, today I'm quite certain that she meant it to be Hitler, but someone said, "That's the mayor, look. She must be in a dispute with the city over her property taxes." In my grandfather's pants pocket, I knew, there was the box with the long matches inside it. I reached a hand into his pocket to take it out. He himself stood there as if thunderstruck for a few long moments and stared at the twisted figure at the top of the pole. We stood and waited for someone to light a match already, but no one dared. Will someone light a match already, what's happened to you, the Belgian neighbor suddenly shrieked, not in French but rather in Yiddish, and angrily flung another bunch of letters at the boards. The pole swayed and almost collapsed. But no one lit the effigy. So he sat there all night, until morning when the tired, sooty firemen stood facing him with hoses and axes.

. . .

A tree planted in the center of a golden field of wheat. The dense wheat reaches up to its trunk. The tree burns down to its roots, but the wheat isn't burning. How can this be? This seems impossible until we see it's not a tree but rather a thin moon, that's not wheat but a sea of small waves, that's not smoke but a cloud of stars.

. . .

Day in and day out he would go to the beach in order to see the sunset. He was addicted to sunsets, a collector of sunsets. The moment in which the sun advanced, suddenly grew, became red, and then the brief span in which it first touches with its tip and is drawn into the water. And of course the final, sudden moment, a drop of red fire, the peak of the sun hesitating another second on the horizon before disappearing. It's possible to hear the sound it makes, like a bubble bursting, like a cigarette you put out in a cup of black coffee. He would announce, "I have a sunset" and run, and once every few years he would succeed in dragging me with him. Back then I didn't get it. And sometimes I would stand there and not look, I would wait for it to be over already. Once I even turned my back to the sea, defiantly. How stupid a person can be, how evil. I remember him standing illuminated in red light, drenched in that light. And once, in his final days, his teeth in a drawer, he said: "All of you is filled with the light of sunset." And truly I was. The sun came through the window of the hospital close to the sea. But he, on the bed, was illuminated in artificial light.

. . .

Our ancestors, *Homo sapiens*, which as you know means "wise man," wiped out, according to one hair-raising conjecture I read about in both Peter Ward and Jared Diamond, the human species closest to them, what we call "Neanderthal Man." Is genocide an appropriate term to describe the interaction of Homo sapiens with the Neanderthals, Peter Ward asks, admitting that we don't know for certain and adding that there are a few things that are perhaps better not to know. What is known for certain is that not long after the appearance of the "wise man" in the regions where Neanderthal Man lived, Neanderthal Man was wiped off the face of the earth. It could be that it's better not to know if 40,000 years ago the first of our kind were involved in the annihilation of those who were of the same species but were apparently a bit different in outward appearance and customs. It's better not to know this, because if this is the case, well, it may be that we have an annihilating impulse in us naturally, much as we have eyes and fingers. Not a murderous impulse, not a death impulse, but rather a mass extinction impulse. After Neanderthal Man became extinct our ancestors took up the extinction of other species. Tens of thousands of years passed. The human species evolved and spread over the face of the earth. We arrived in Siberia, Holland, we crossed the continental pass between Siberia and Alaska on foot, a pass that was open in the time of the last ice age and closed due to climate changes approximately 14,000 years ago. Finally we arrived in North America and Canada and there met mammoths and mastodons that had lived there undisturbed for almost a million and a half years. About 12,000 years ago we arrived in America as guests, and after a thousand or two thousand years the large animals were extinct, species whose dominion in that place lasted, as mentioned, a million and a half years, and were obliterated from the face of the continent in no time at all. With spears and sharp stone knives we wiped out the ancient elephants. In opposition to the argument that perhaps they went extinct due to climate change, Jared Diamond raises a particular objection: How is it that the mammoths and the rest of the animals that went extinct then had survived a million and a half years of extreme changes in climate, and then, of all things, it's the *human summer*, if we can call it that, that they don't, in the end, survive? The extinction of the ice-age mammals is enough in itself to convict the human species; were we to go extinct today, this would be nothing more than historic justice, prehistoric justice to be exact. This sentence too is an expression of the human extinction impulse and perhaps it would be better if it were expunged. Reasonable doubt might convince our attorney, but in court such a flimsy defense won't help at all. Luckily, this court will never be convened, unless, perhaps, I thought after a moment on my bench, in the pre-morning cold, unless it actually will be convened, I mean maybe it already has been convened, maybe it's already sitting in judgment. Diamond points out that the annihilation of the large mammals in America and Australia was one of the causes of the native cultures' annihilation in these places by the European invaders thousands of years later. Without the possibility of domesticating large beasts, the Indians and Aborigines, who had insisted on annihilating the large animals in their midst, didn't have beasts of burden or beasts for food, wool, and milk, and thus were easy prey for the European beast masters, who were immune to the diseases that they brought with them in their cattle, which hadn't been annihilated, diseases that wiped out the local inhabitants in Australia and America, who were not immune. We annihilated the mammoths in America and the giant kangaroo in Australia, to pick just two from among hundreds and thousands of species, and the knowledge we amassed in so doing has been very successfully put into practice upon our own kind. We annihilated Neanderthal Man, why not annihilate the Jews as well. I'll stop here, but the list goes on, and the court will be presented with this list in a thick binder accompanied by photographs. The Spaniards and the rest of the conquerors who arrived in America continued what the early Americans had started ten thousand years before them, annihilation of the locals: person, plant, and animal. These great deeds may be hidden from our eyes, but in court the prosecutor will present the evidence and will without doubt bring about our criminal convictions. It's clear there's no real need for a trial, in fact; we ourselves are already busy carrying out the sentence, which can only be a sentence of death. We only know two things for certain about the ice-age humans, writes Peter Ward in *The Call of Distant Mammoths*: They knew how to kill large animals and they knew how to roam great distances. Traveling far and killing, I think to myself, hooray, our ancient legacy is still with us, the airplane and the slaughterhouse are still popular tools. I can only point out that I myself have chosen not to kill large animals and not to roam great distances. When I can sit in one place, I sit in one place, and I prefer this bench, I thought when I laid down on it that same night, to the endless plains, the plains of southern Canada full of "big game" animals, as they're called. In any case, I don't roam in order to kill big animals and I don't play the big game. I don't roam in order to kill small animals either. Each morning I get up at 5:30 and feed vegetables to Bob the guinea pig and clear his corner of the porch with a teaspoon. If I remember a dream that I dreamed, I tell it to him, for instance the dream in which I see three women poets dressed in white and wearing straw hats who split a large plate of lamb cutlets at the festival of poets and complain about the state of poetry and the decline of the peace movement in Israel. Indeed, this wasn't a dream, I saw it with my own eyes. With my own ears I heard the poets at the festival of poets pass a platter of spicy beef sausages one to another and light imported cigarettes for each other. The cattle were imprisoned, the cattle were slaughtered, the cattle were sliced up and frozen, the cattle were placed on the table of the three senior poets, one of whom had won the Bialik Prize, and so in a certain sense were placed on the table of Hebrew poetry as well, where it met with the poets' sharp, glimmering teeth, the teeth of poetry. I stared at them and thought that, to tell the truth, I'm not interested in reading the rhymes of meat-eating poets, I'm not interested in watching the comedies of meat-eating playwrights, which are always monstrous comedies, and I'm not interested in the prose of meat-eaters, which is always the cruel prose of slaughters, slaughterers who pretend they're knitting lace at dusk to the strains of a harp. Ward points out that among the stone tools of people from the last ice age we often find weapons made of stones that were excavated hundreds of kilometers from the places they were made. The arms trade and weapons trafficking were already flourishing in 10,000 BCE. Spears were imported from Siberia to North America in order to annihilate the wooly mammoth, this fact places our humanity in a new light. It's possible we didn't have a choice, it's possible that the hunger was overwhelming, it's possible that in order to live we had to kill everything we could lay our hands on. The Russian tank that was imported from Dnipropetrovsk to the Golan Heights and painted the colors of the Syrian flag and struck my uncle's tank, which was imported from the United States, and the spear that was imported from Dnipropetrovsk to Seattle and killed a young mammoth, I don't see a big difference between them. The spear and the cannon of a tank look so similar to me that I can see my uncle killed by a spear whose tip is made from sharpened stone, and a mammoth killed by a well-targeted strike from a Soviet tank painted the colors of the Syrian flag—red, white, and black, with two green stars. Two months after my uncle was killed, my brother was born, and he was named after him, Shalom (that is, "peace"). When I was a child, I didn't like the name Shalom, and I distorted it every way possible, until one of the nicknames I made up, Shalki, almost became my brother's official name, and after he turned eighteen he went to the Ministry of the Interior to change the name on his identity card once and for all. But the clerk at the Ministry of the Interior in Netanya knew our family and my uncle, and he firmly refused to change my brother's name. In front of my brother's eyes, he angrily tore up the form and stuffed it in his mouth.

. . .

He would lie on the beach in Netanya for hours, and would return red on one side and covered in sand on the other. They thought he enjoyed the hot sand, but no, he stayed there too long for mere enjoyment. He would listen closely, as it were, like a burglar. A few minutes before five he would get up and go to the lifeguard stand to read the names of Holocaust survivors. Every day at five in the afternoon a worker would come with a broom dunked in clear glue and stick the list onto the lifeguard stand. He traveled to Poland in 1949, and in the same year traveled to Germany, but what befell him on that journey we do not know. We know nothing except that a few days after he returned from Poland, he traveled to the house of the poet Uri Zvi Grinberg bearing news from Lvov. He didn't make an appointment but just showed up at Grinberg's house in Ramat Gan. He got lost for two days on the way from Netanya to Ramat Gan. He fell asleep on one bus and afterward got on the wrong bus, though he'd explicitly asked whether it was the bus to Ramat Gan, and the driver had clearly answered "yes," even though he hadn't heard the question, and hurried to close the doors, and he fell asleep again, and accidentally arrived in Jerusalem. He thought he was dreaming, after all the way is so short and he knew the way but despite this he still found himself so far away. He'd almost run out of money, he slept on a street bench, and the next day hitchhiked back to Netanya, waving his red National Health Service credentials, and people stopped for him immediately. He didn't give up, stubbornly bought a new ticket and again got on the 641 and the bus immediately started on its way, was really sailing along, but then the radiator burst, and all the passengers were transferred to another bus, which was going not to Ramat Gan, but to Ramat Chen instead. When he arrived at the poet's house two days later he was already filthy and exhausted, with bad breath. In an interview with literary scholar Dan Miron, Grinberg would eventually tell how he finally made up his mind to publish the poems in *The Streets of the River* following that same meeting with my grandfather. My grandfather told me about his meeting with Grinberg after the poet's funeral, which we both attended. This was shortly after the capture of my neighbor, the kidnapper of the boy, in the year 1981. I write here the little I recall from what my grandfather told me. So many years have passed since then. Grinberg opened the door for my grandfather in a three-piece suit, with a pipe in his mouth. My grandfather was also wearing a three-piece suit, but one that was horribly wrinkled after two days of buses and travel. My grandfather also had a pipe in his mouth. My grandfather introduced himself, and Grinberg—as it became clear, some time later—mistakenly thought that standing before him was the Yiddish poet Zvi Burstein, author of the *Golden Star*, and cordially invited him in. Grinberg filled my grandfather's pipe before he filled his own, and then offered my grandfather the large metal lighter he still kept from the days of his service in the Austro-Hungarian army in World War I. My grandfather looked at the metal lighter and said to him, an Austro-Hungarian lighter, and Grinberg replied, I saw a soldier light it and get shot, at night. At night. The flame ignites for a moment, Grinberg said, and the enemy waits, and between the flame of the lighter and the first spark from the tip of the cigarette a bullet is fired in your direction. I saw young men eighteen years old die in the blink of an eye between taking out their lighters and the first drags from their cigarettes. The lighter falls and the cigarette falls and you bend down carefully and pick the cigarette up off the ground and smoke it, and the lighter, Grinberg said and placed the lighter on the small glass table next to him, the lighter you clean with your shirttail and take for yourself. I heard the sound of a machine gun, Grinberg said to my grandfather, I heard the screams and you couldn't tell who was screaming. On the bank of the river. I lowered my head into the mud and lit my pipe, Grinberg said, and removed his pipe from his mouth. From the poet's open mouth, my grandfather told me, thick smoke billowed forth. Grinberg asked my grandfather to read to him from his Yiddish poems, and my grandfather, who was surprised by this request, said that he had never written Yiddish poetry. Grinberg didn't understand why the Yiddish poet Zvi Burstein was claiming he is not a Yiddish poet, but he kept quiet. They sat and smoked for a long time and then Grinberg said to him, in truth, I understand, I too never wrote Yiddish poetry, Yiddish poetry is impossible to write because it is impossible to speak in Yiddish any longer. Yes. How can we speak in a nonexistent language, Grinberg asked my grandfather, and tapped his fingernail twice against the cross engraved on the metal lighter, how can we speak in burned letters. They conversed, of course, in

Yiddish. My grandfather, who was amazed by this strange pronouncement from the great poet, was embarrassed and didn't know how to respond. Only a long while later, when the room was already full of smoke, did Grinberg ask my grandfather what he actually wanted and why he'd come to his home late at night. My grandfather asked permission to go wash his face in the sink, and Grinberg followed my grandfather with his eyes as he walked down the hallway until he was swallowed up by the first door on the right. When my grandfather returned, his face washed and his hair combed by Grinberg's steel comb, which he found next to the sink, he told Grinberg that upon his return from his trip to Poland and Germany he had made up his mind to bequeath all his possessions to the poet as a gift—his share of the Hotel Tel Aviv and all the money he'd saved from his carpentry work, and his tools and furniture as well. Possessions and even the word "possessions" were putting him into such a deep depression that he almost couldn't bear to carry a wallet. Possessions seemed like leprosy to him, and he had to get rid of the leprosy, he said, scratch it from his skin. A man buys an apartment and fills it with furniture, and then! he said. He had already approached a lawyer who had prepared the gift deed for him. My grandfather took out the deed before the amazed eyes of Grinberg, surrounded in smoke, the deed in which were detailed all his bequeathed possessions, down to every last hammer, as well as the declaration that everything had been bequeathed of his own free will and with no conditions. As a sort of prelude, my grandfather removed a bundle of poetry books from the leather bag that he'd dragged with him on those buses, and set it down on the poet's table. There, my grandfather told me from memory, were Alterman's *Stars Outside*; Shlonsky's *Rough Stones*; the manuscript of Vogel's *Before the Dark Gate*, which he'd received as a gift from Vogel himself, who had been a tenant in our hotel; Leah Goldberg's *Smoke Rings*; and Uri Zvi Grinberg's *A Great Fear and the Moon*. He didn't deliver the news from Lvov, and when I was informed many years later what the news was, I understood why he didn't deliver it, and at the sight of the photographs that I found in my grandfather's estate in an envelope labeled "News from Lvov" years later, I began shivering so severely that I took the old blanket from astronomy class out of my closet and wrapped myself up inside. I wrap myself up in this blanket whenever I start to shiver, and I do tend to get the shivers from time to time, after all I live in the State of Israel. I got the shivers there on my bench along the boulevard as well, and wished for that same blanket, but it was upstairs, in my closet, under heavy crates, inside a suitcase. Grinberg stared at the pile of books that got taller and taller on the table, book after book, and at the deed, upon which his name, Uri Zvi Grinberg, was written as the recipient, in the name of the grantor, Zvi Burstein. I'll write an IOU, my grandfather announced, and Grinberg repeated like an echo, an IOU. It was my grandfather's intention to bequeath to the poet his portion of the hotel and all the rest of his possessions, down to the last sock, "including the holes," since he was firm in his decision to rid himself of all his possessions and after thorough consideration understood that in the entire country there wasn't a man more deserving of his possessions than Uri Zvi Grinberg. He removed his watch, the same watch belonging to his brother that he'd brought from Poland, and placed it like a weight upon the book *A Great Fear and the Moon*, which my grandmother had bought in her youth in Berlin. I searched for someone to bequeath my possessions to, and it was clear to me that an intellectual would have to receive my possessions, since only in the hands of an intellectual will my possessions cease to be possessions. And if an intellectual, then why not a poet, and if a poet, then who else but Uri Zvi Grinberg, my grandfather said to Uri Zvi Grinberg. You can come live in our hotel in Netanya as soon as the transfer of ownership is in order. There are also some gold rings that the "Old

Man" brought from Germany, and there's also this money sewn into overcoats, I'll give you anything that turns up. Grinberg was very upset. He couldn't accept the gift, but refusing it would be impolite. In his confusion he opened up the book by Leah Goldberg and began leafing through it, and then he read aloud the first poem in the collection to my grandfather. When he finished reading, a troubling silence prevailed. Grinberg got up and stood next to a window, and my grandfather told me that he then noticed that in the poet's courtyard stood a shed of some sort, a shed quite like the carpentry shed in the courtyard of the hotel in Netanya, and while Grinberg's residence was totally dark, the shed was illuminated from within by a powerful light, to the point that it was hard to look at it directly. Grinberg leaned his forehead on the cold glass. His pipe had gone out and the smoke dissipated. So they remained, without saying a word for some time. The sound of a child's cough rose from one of the rooms. Someone spoke in his sleep. There they were, Grinberg next to the window and my grandfather in an armchair, until there was a knock at the door. It was my grandmother, who'd found a stencil copy of the deed, read it, and understood what it was about and where her husband had disappeared to. Grinberg's address on Marganit Street in Ramat Gan was printed under his name on the contract, and she'd ordered a special taxi from Netanya to Ramat Gan. It took her only forty minutes to make the trip. For a moment she stood there in the entranceway to the house, next to the emaciated olive tree the poet had planted, a copy of the deed in her hand, and then she went inside. The door wasn't locked, and my grandfather and Grinberg turned and saw her standing under the dim light above the door and holding her copies of the papers in both hands. A moment later the taxi honked and disturbed the calm of the night. A small boy, wrapped in a blanket, appeared in the hallway with eyes closed.

They sat in the back seat of the taxi while the driver got lost in the small side streets. Remorseful, my grandfather was hesitant to disclose to my grandmother that he had left books of poetry—that is, *her* books of poetry—on Grinberg's glass table, including her Leah Goldberg, who was my grandmother's close friend and a regular guest of the Hotel Tel Aviv and is even pictured there in a well-known photograph, smoking on the balcony of her usual room and smiling at the flowers, and her Alterman too, which was my grandmother's favorite book and had even been inscribed to her by the young poet, who was a regular guest of the hotel in the mid-thirties and even stood as my "godfather" at my *bris*, in the year 1970, a ceremony at which S. Y. Agnon was also present, a short time before the death of all three—Goldberg, Alterman, and Agnon. The whole matter of the deed and the books was almost the end of the marriage. As a matter of fact, they even presented themselves before the rabbinate, seeking a divorce, but the judge, who was a townsman of my grandfather, refused to perform the ceremony, and so they returned shamefaced to the hotel. My grandfather removed the cork from a dark, cold bottle. And approximately two years later, their youngest son, my uncle Shalom, was born, of whom I've already spoken.

Years later, when Grinberg's time came and he lay in a nursing home in the same room as the artist and writer Nachum Gutman, my grandfather took me to visit him. A few small books were resting on the chest of drawers next to his bed. Grinberg was very thin and all that was left of his red hair were a few gray ones. Spots covered his skin and the lenses of his glasses were cloudy. On the way there, we heard it announced on the radio that the kidnapper and murderer of the missing child had been caught and they said the name of the accused, whom I call here Fabian Zachariah, and I wanted to tell my grandfather that we had a neighbor on the fifth floor of our building with that name, but I kept quiet. When Grinberg saw us from his bed, he made a fist to greet us, and even though there's no doubt he failed to recognize us (of course he didn't recognize me, he had never met me before), he waved to us happily as he would have to old friends. Nachum Gutman was fast asleep in the bed at the other end of the room, and one of his paintings, *The Watermelon Eater*, was hanging next to his bed, along its length. My grandfather approached Grinberg, bent over him, and kissed his cheek. From my place I saw that Grinberg was wiggling the toes of his bare feet. My grandfather looked through the books on the chest of drawers a bit. "Do you remember this watch, Drorik?" my grandfather asked me, and pointed at the half-opened drawer, in which medications and creams and other belongings were scattered about in disarray. I didn't understand what he was talking about, but since I was getting more and more upset about the news that had been broadcast on the bus radio, at which the other passengers had actually and spontaneously broken out in thunderous applause, I didn't even ask what he meant. But I went over, peeked at the watch in the drawer, and compared the time on it with my own watch. The watch in the drawer was perfectly accurate. I remember that the time was exactly three o'clock, and that next to the watch, in the half-open drawer, rested a pair of dice, a few large coins, different types of medications, *The Book of the Zohar* fastened shut with a knotted shoelace, a plastic comb with a few broken teeth, and a few old photographs, among which was a photograph of the young Grinberg in a suit and wearing a hat at rakish angle, standing next to the poet Chaim Nachman Bialik, whom I recognized, he in a hat worn straight, and upon which were two fountain pens, bound together with a rubber band.

. . .

At the age of eighty, in opposition to his doctor's warning, my grandfather met us on Netanya's limestone cliff, near the mini-golf course, in order to celebrate his birthday and fulfill his old dream—to fly. He always dreamed he was flying at a low altitude, just a few centimeters above the ground. My dreams of flight were also like that. I dreamed that I changed my form from a bat to a praying mantis to a bird. Apparently a sparrow: my namesake. If I have a favorite bird, it would have to be the house sparrow. I too dreamed about low flight. Every time I dreamed about flying high, above the clouds, the dream would end with my falling, my grandfather said to me or I said to him. In Netanya the rental of various kinds of paragliders was already flourishing, and at least two companies were offering gliding services for senior citizens who had adequate insurance coverage. The flying elderly of Netanya even ran in the municipal elections and as you may have heard won two seats on the city council, though they did nothing for their voting public. Almost every day, and especially on weekends, it was possible to look at flocks upon flocks of colorful hang gliders sailing over Netanya's beach and cliffs, and at old people in the air waving their walking sticks, from which they refused to be separated, above the luminous waves. All of us arrived—my grandfather, my father, my mother, my two brothers, and I—at the edge of the cliff at five in the morning. My grandfather approached one of the people renting paragliders, who was sleeping in a tent sewn out of a paraglider that had ripped while he was flying it and had almost been the death of him—or so he told every customer. The man surveyed us drowsily and between yawns hitched us up, the six of us, to our respective oversized wings. We stood there bewildered. Gusts of wind from the sea lifted us a few centimeters off the ground and we grabbed onto shrubs and short cords that were tied to metal poles precisely for this purpose. "Like chickens," my grandfather declared impatiently, and positioned himself facing the sea, ten centimeters from the cliff's edge, while holding his hat to keep the wind from snatching it. Without warning, as though he were sleepwalking, my younger brother Tomer took two or three steps forward. Our fate was sealed. Wind from the direction of the sea immediately answered him, grabbed him, and lifted him up a bit, and soon he was flying above the shoreline below us, apparently still fast asleep, for he neither made a sound nor waved to us. My brother Shalom glided over to save him. Quickly my father and mother joined in as well, gliding after my younger brother, who had woken up in the meantime and was staring down at the sea right under his nose as if there was no sight more natural than this.

I remained on the cliff with my grandfather, barely staying put on the gravelly limestone soil, struggling with the wind pulling at the underside of my orange wings. "Fly, fly, here's your chance," my grandfather said. "And what's with you?" I asked. "I'm about to go, in a moment, I'm only taking a blood-pressure pill first," he said and patted his many pockets. "I'll be the last." I reached out to point at the pocket where he kept his medications, but in my haste released my grip on the low shrub. The wind, whose direction had changed all of a sudden, now blowing almost vertically, took me immediately, and flew me above the roofs of the hotels. I spun like the blades of a propeller. My socks were dunked in the clouds, or perhaps those were the wet sheets on the hotel roofs. I saw a family sitting around a plastic table on the roof of the Four Seasons hotel playing rummy cub. Their francs were piled up under cups of café au lait. White rectangular stones were positioned on the table next to the butter. I saw the light of the sun reflected in the solar panels—in all the solar panels on each and every hotel. I saw a band of black birds rise out of black foliage. I saw my father seemingly approach the sun and my mother touch the foam of the waves with her bare toes. Since then I have glided there alone many times. After a few minutes, I had completed my circuit above the beach and glided toward the sea. My parents and two brothers were languidly flying here and there, one behind the other, as though they were already experts, like a man who after a few minutes in the water understands how to float and whistles smugly at the clouds.

The temptation is great to write how grandfather, eighty years old, flew next to them, or how he lay on the sands below, after a short dive and crash. But that's not how it happened. He only stood there, in his green wings, close to the cliff's edge, and looked at us gliding, drawing close and drifting away, descending almost to the water's surface, ascending until it was nearly impossible to see us or at least distinguish us from the birds. And a half hour later the man renting the paragliders rang a large bell to signal that that was it. Our shoulders aching from the harnesses, we directed ourselves toward the landing strip marked out by bottles filled with sea sand next to the pitiful tent, and finally touched ground, or rather touched sand, coming to a stop on an old spring mattress that was placed perpendicular to the ground. My grandfather was still standing there, looking out at the horizon, his hands still holding his hat so it wouldn't fly off. His cane had been dropped at his side. We went looking for a café to celebrate his birthday. But they were all closed.

. . .

"A rhinoceros once passed through our town. He escaped from the Saxony Circus—well-known in Zwickau, Germany—crossed the eastern border, and continued across Poland. No one noticed it. Until it passed through our streets. No one among us had ever seen an animal like that. My father approached and rolled a white cabbage at it. In two or three bites, the rhinoceros ate the cabbage. This is what I remember of my father. So, there—you asked, I answered you." (When he stood on a platform in the East Warsaw train station in 1934, his father suddenly knelt down before him, and to his great embarrassment—a policeman blew into his steel whistle—lowered the sock on his left foot, brought his lips to his ankle, and tried to kiss the short, protruding bone.)

. . .

He signed up for a trip for "Senior Citizens of the Religious Community," a cruise around the coast of Africa (three glatt kosher meals a day and a cantorial concert in Cape Town). A hundred old people wandering around Africa, he said when he returned, as if life had led them only to this, to photograph the beaches of Djibouti and to vomit across from Madagascar. Whose idea was this! I'm already an eighty-five-year-old Jew! On the ship itself, all these beautiful Jews, the plump, bourgeois Jews, with their beautiful pensions, the Jews of silk and velvet, the Jews of Shemini Atzeret, the Jews of armchairs and galoshes (someone on the deck took out a pair of opera glasses and saw my grandfather standing on the beach, after he surreptitiously got off the boat, a stowaway escaping onto dry land, to his left the elephant). Did I tell you about the elephant that passed through our village? And about my father, who fed it cabbage? On the boat I met a man from the same city as me, not "shtetl," *city*, for you all of Poland is shtetls, for you Lublin is a shtetl, Warsaw a shtetl, Krakow—a remote shtetl; even Moscow is a shtetl, only Tel Aviv is a city, yes, a big city, metropolitan . . . and Netanya too, yes . . . anyway, I met this Jew there, and perhaps I even remembered him from Ciechanów, but no, not really, I had no intention of remembering. He wanted to reminisce about childhood, and I said *no childhood memories*. He said, but how? And I answered, no. He said, but there are, and I answered, blot them out. Nevertheless, we exchanged a few words and he remembered the rhinoceros and he remembered Father and he remembered the cabbage. He told me that he's lived in Peru twenty years already, and he brought a small animal with him for the cruise, which I didn't recognize then, but today I know that it was a cavy, or guinea pig, or sea pig as I've heard the Germans call it, but that's a stupid name, it's not a pig and not a sea, cavy, it's a cavy, why make everything a pig? Imagine them calling a sparrow a winged pig! What? Or the honey pig! The bee! Nonsense! It whistled for me, I petted it. You've never seen such a simple animal in your life. The Peruvian Jew brought his cavy in order to release it into the jungle. He planned to get off the ship in Beira, which is in Mozambique, he said, during the planned nighttime anchorage, and not return. He had already done it before, of course he'd done it before. Many times a year he escapes from these pleasure cruises, he said, and the crew gives up and continues sailing without him, while he's already penetrated deep into the continent with his cavy in a ventilated cage, which appears, for the sake of camouflage, like a broad suitcase. He travels the world with cavies he raises near Lima, and releases them. And then the Peruvian Jew looked here and there to see if anyone could see us, my grandfather said, and revealed another cavy, which was in the cage, gnawing on lettuce. A white cavy, with a forelock, your heart went out to it, my grandfather said. He scatters this species around the whole world. Within a number of months a couple of cavies will multiple and become a population of a few dozen cavies, and after a few years—a good hundred or two, the Peruvian Jew said to me in his funny Yiddish . . . The cavy nodded as if in agreement and ate a green pepper in delight. These are the most wonderful animals on the face of the earth. This is the true crown of creation. Harmless and yet providing so much loving affection. Big cowards, but after they overcome their fear, they devote all their love, which is the other side of fear, to you and you alone. They yawn and expose their teeth and sometimes lick your finger. Only on rare occasions are their black eyes closed. Most of them are white, black, or chestnut colored. Their hearing is very sharp, and they love to hide in small, dark places. They whistle when they want to be fed—or when they're frightened. When I return home, said the Peruvian Jew, my cavies hear the sound of my steps in the distance and whistle to me happily. Sometimes they gnash their teeth, and when they're hot they huddle around a bottle full of frozen water I put out for them during the warm season in Lima. You see, they have long, thin mustaches, and hair jutting out on all sides, which seems unjustified, as it were, but which makes them look almost imposing, just as his mustache did for my younger brother, who fled to the Soviet Union when I fled to Peru, the Jew said. Perhaps they aren't the smartest animals on earth according to human standards, but I love these cavies more than any person I've ever met, and certainly more than a few supposed friends, he said. Almost every month I travel to a different country and release them into a nature preserve, in couples or groups of four, usually in groups of eight, he said, and lifted the edge of some cloth that was covering another basket in which six more cavies, perhaps ten even, were napping, my grandfather said. All this is strange, I know, said the Jew from Peru. All the money I earned selling insurance to the arms industry I exhaust in their care and release. My children have already sued me, claimed that I'm gnawing away at their inheritance, but I won of course. The love I feel for these creatures exceeds the limits of societal logic, without a doubt. I know that some of them will be devoured in the places to which I bring them, but nevertheless, those places are their proper home. They eat almost only vegetables, and they know how to hide. Look at these short legs, look at these sharp ears, why even a tail they don't have, said the Jew in his strange Yiddish, and tears came to his eyes. They gnaw on boards in order to sharpen their teeth and leave a lot of droppings, and I collect them with a teaspoon and place them in flowerpots. Each one has a name and a nickname. And all this time a British Jew was sitting next to us on the deck, my grandfather said, and from time to time removed his pipe from between his teeth and without saying a thing pointed at the waves and the distant shore of southeast Africa. True, said the Peruvian Jew, they bite me sometimes, but their teeth are very small and you can barely feel it, it's like a caress. But look, it's not easy, my crusade, and I'm getting more and more tired. Perhaps it's insignificant, but I'm already an eighty-five year-old Jew. Twenty-seven years I've been dealing with the cavies, scattering them and scattering them some more. Where haven't I been? I started with us of course, in Peru. Afterward I moved to Brazil, and after that to Honduras, to Guatemala, to Uruguay, to Argentina, to northern Chile. After that I began sailing the seas. Twenty kilometers outside Lima I have a small farm and I raise them there and prepare them for the crucial journey. I have a loyal employee. A Lithuanian Jew. When I return from a cruise, new pups are already awaiting me. There's room there for everyone, but I already know that I won't manage to release all of them, since they multiple so quickly, and I—well, my strength is waning. I can release so few, all told, he said in a whisper, perhaps two to three each month, and with his cane he raised the edge of his blanket and revealed a large cage with about thirty cavies inside. The journey isn't easy for them, but after a week of crowding, they have all the space they could want. Of course, I can't control them after they go out into the wild, he said, but I hope for their sake that they don't flee every which way, breaking up the family, but instead gather together in one place. Strange, you know, back in Poland there weren't animals, maybe a few goats and that woman, Ge, Ge, c'mon, what was she called, Gesya, had one chicken . . . but my grandfather repeated to him, no, no childhood reminiscing, but since you've already said Gesya, know that her name wasn't Gesya, but Genya instead, everyone got it wrong, called her Gesya, but I knew what her real name was. And it wasn't Gesya, definitely not Gesya, but Genya instead, and she didn't have a chicken, you've got it all wrong, but a rooster instead, for certain. The ship anchored, my grandfather continued, and we went down to the shore intending to return twenty-four hours later, but the Peruvian Jew had other plans. The porters were already waiting for him on the shore, and they boarded the ship and helped him to roll a type of small, two-wheeled wooden wagon off of it. He waved good-bye to me. I disembarked after him and walked a bit on dry land after almost a week at sea. I fell, in fact, the ground was so firm. I lay there, on this African shore, and suddenly I was struck by the strong suspicion that all of this was a dream. Zvi Burstyn in Africa, I said to myself, c'mon, really. He said Burstyn and he wrote Burstyn, whereas we said Burstein and wrote Burstein. I fell there on the shore of Zimbabwe and blackness washed over me, I thought it wouldn't pass, it went on and on and I understood it was a stroke, the word stroke actually crossed my mind like a scorpion, but the Peruvian Jew was suddenly next to me and grabbed me with both hands under my armpits and pulled me back up. Forget it, forget it, c'mon Moishe, I said to him. Under a shady tree I saw his horde napping in the hay. I had a carrot in my pocket, I asked him if they like carrots. You should have seen what kind of smile came over his face. He truly started walking on air. And he let me feed them, and I fed them. There was a nature preserve, and a few elephants were standing there. They stood and swept up sand with their trunks and tossed it on their own backs and on each other's backs. They stood there in their slow rhythm and in their slow rhythm they bent down and gathered sand and tossed it on their backs like they were rinsing in it. The air was full of sand floating like snow. I knew that once I had been in this fine snow. I stepped over to the elephants. They moved to clear some space for me. I let go of my suitcase and newspaper. The suitcase was trampled and the wind snatched the newspaper. I had a few more carrots in my pocket. One of the elephants gathered a handful of sand in his trunk and tossed it on my back and on my head.

. . .

Was there a small earthquake? The bench shook under me, that night, and it seemed that it moved from its place, burrowing into the sand and advancing, clearing a path for itself to the north as if it was a wooden ship on a sand cruise. From upstream the porters waved good-bye to our townsman, who bent down and released his cavies at the spot where the plain ends and the jungle starts and rises up all at once, and they bolted to the dense vegetation, whistling loudly, and then disappeared, to a man, jumping into the green underbrush like dolphins into ocean waves. The Brit made his way through some giant flowers and with his pipe pointed out each and every flower and one cavy, black-white-chestnut, which dashed under my bench, leapt to the other bank, and returned to the open cage of the Peruvian Jew, who noticed him and said, in surprise, "She came back to me." My grandfather made his way through the elephants' thick legs, advancing next to them, dusty like them, moving his ears, holding a crushed suitcase in his hand. Everyone turned and disappeared up the stairs of the synagogue at 22 Smuts Boulevard, and I heard my grandfather say to the leader of the herd, "*Mincha*, afternoon prayers." My grandfather and the leader of the herd went in to pray and the rest of the group waited in the synagogue's rear courtyard, under the quince and lemon trees, under their scent. From inside, the sound of prayer and joy burst forth. The elephant flipped through his prayer book, moistened his thumb with spit. Shofar blasts arose from the courtyard.

. . .

- I remember the old, heavy telephone handsets as barbells. I loved to place the earpiece on the base slowly and carefully, as if the entire telephone were made of glass. And sometimes as soon as I put it down the telephone would ring again.

- I remember how everything was wrapped in tinfoil.
- I remember a bathtub full of Pyrex instruments.
- I remember the center back for Maccabi Netanya, the football/soccer club, Chaim Bar, crossing the street in his Sabbath clothes and stopping suddenly.
- When we would travel on a straight road I would sometimes ask, "Is this the Ruler Road?" Most of the time they told me it was.
- I remember a place called the Star of the Jordan, you could see everything from there. Everything.
- "Yes, it's scary," he said to me, and bowed his head. "But don't be scared."
- I remember someone told me that whoever licks stamps with his tongue poisons himself a bit with each letter he sends.

. . .

They returned from the East Warsaw train station by horse and wagon. The trip lasted more than two hours. They got off at the main street and walked a bit on foot. He touched his pocket then, and inside was the printed train schedule. He was alarmed because he'd wanted to give his son the schedule. So he would have it. He looked at his watch. In another five or six minutes the train would depart. He stopped and then continued walking. She didn't notice that he had stopped. He crushed the schedule between his fingers. They arrived home. 35 Warszawska Street, Ciechanów. He asked his wife what's for lunch.

JB ... 391 . 70

COMITÉ INTERNATIONAL DE LA CROIX-ROUGE

Palais du Conseil Général

GENÈVE (Suisse)

DEMANDEUR — NADAWCA — ANFRAGESTELLER

Nom - *Nazwisko* - *Name* Bursztejn

Prénom - *Imię* - *Vorname* Zwi

Rue - *Ulica* - *Strasse* 70 Gorenrajch

Localité - *Miejscowość* - *Ortschaft* Raanana

Province - *Województwo* - *Provinz*

Pays - *Kraj* - *Land* Palestine

Message à transmettre — Zlecenie — Mitteilung

(25 mots au maximum, nouvelles de caractère strictement personnel et familial) — (*najwyżej 25 słów, wiadomości ściśle osobiste*) — (*nicht über 25 Worte nur persönliche Familiennachrichten*).

Date - *Data* - *Datum*

DESTINATAIRE — ODBIORCA — EMPFÄNGER

Nom - *Nazwisko* - *Name* Bursztejn

Prénom - *Imię* - *Vorname* Szlama

Lieu et date de naissance *Miejsce i data urodzenia* *Geburtsort und Datum*

Fils de *Imię ojca* *Sohn des* et de *Imię matki* *und des*

Dernière adresse connue *Ostatni adres* *Letztbekannte Adresse*

Rue - *Ulica* - *Strasse* Ul. Warszawska 35, 90612

Localité - *Miejscowość* - *Ortschaft* Ciechanow Maz.

Province - *Województwo* - *Provinz* SUD OST PREUSSEN 29 AVR. 1940

Pays - *Kraj* - *Land* DEUTSCHLAND

RÉPONSE AU VERSO. Ecrire très lisiblement. — **ODPOWIEDŹ NA ODWROCIE.** Pisać czytelnie. — **ANTWORT UMSEITIG.** Bitte deutlich schreiben.

RÉPONSE **ODPOWIEDŻ** **ANTWORT**

Message à renvoyer au demandeur — Zlecenie dla nadawcy — Mitteilung an den Anfragesteller zurückzusenden

(25 mots au maximum, nouvelles de caractère strictement personnel et familial) — (*najwyżej 25 słów, wiadomości ściśle osobiste*) — (*nicht über 25 Worte, nur persönliche Familiennachrichten*).

Date - *Data* - *Datum*: 17.IV 1940 J.

Wir leben alle. Abram Idel zu hause. Jakob in Tikocin ul. Pilsudzkiego 20 Riwka Braun bei Bialystok schreib zu ihm, auch zu Tante Toba. Ciechanower in Fridman leben

66

Prière d'écrire très lisiblement. **Pisać bardzo wyraźnie.** **Bitte sehr deutlich schreiben**

. . .

In a letter bearing the stamp of the Red Cross and dated April 17, 1940 (it was only sent on the 29th of the month because it had to pass before the scrutinizing eye of the censor), the father of my grandfather reports in garbled German ("Please, write very clearly," is printed at the bottom of the letter, in German, Polish, and French)—or, anyway, this is as much as I can decipher—"Everyone is alive. Abram is at home. Jakob is in Tikocin on Piłsudski Street. Riwka Braun is near Bialystok. Write him, also to Aunt Tova. In Ciechanów live free." The father of my grandfather, he who fed the rhinoceros cabbage, wrote these lines. A man rolls cabbage to an escaped rhinoceros, and twenty or thirty years later finds himself writing a letter that's like a last will. Not a thing remains of him other than a piece of air mail, an old family picture, and the cabbage he placed before the rhinoceros, an animal that rolled from Africa to a German zoo, and from there escaped eastward and was never caught. Like many living creatures, the father of my grandfather was annihilated by the super predator of his time. During the Permian period the super predator was the Gorgonopsia, a sort of long-fanged, giant lizard. Peter Ward writes about him in his book *Gorgon*. During the Cretaceous period it was the Tyrannosaurus Rex, and in the middle of the twentieth century it was the German war machine, which in place of long fangs developed armaments, tanks, and planes, until it too was annihilated by powers stronger than itself. I wrote that not a thing remains of my grandfather's father, yet the hand writing these lines actually refutes that rash assertion. He wrote the letter in broken German, and in fact began writing this book with his fountain pen that day. A pen waits seventy years and then finishes writing, even though the pen is not in my possession, that pen is buried somewhere in Poland along with many more pens.

The soil of Poland is drenched in ink. The last words written by that pen were the Red Cross letter. My grandfather's father wrote the letter that is stamped with the Red Cross's stamp, and this stamp is the logo as it were for these lines. To this very day I hear the thump of the stamp on the paper, I hear it now as if it were stamped on my head, as if the stamp were dipped in red ink and forcibly impressed on my forehead. My grandfather's father began writing these lines written here in crooked letters in the year 1940; in my opinion there's nothing about this that's hard to understand. His handwriting resembles my handwriting. My grandfather's father, Shlomo Burstein (not to be confused with my grandmother's father, Shlomo Goldring), a man I never once met and who was murdered about thirty years before my birth, he is my ghostwriter. This is the correct order: my grandfather's immigration certificate (1934)—his father's Red Cross letter (1940)—the gift deed from my grandfather to Grinberg (1949)—my grandfather's tenure letter (1959), which we'll get to shortly—and then my birth certificate (1970). There were many other stops on this trail of documents, naturally, and there will be many more. Here I'm merely pointing out the general direction. My grandfather's father became extinct in a mass extinction, but these lines by their very existence deny that extinction, deny the possibility of extinction. The Vietnamese Zen teacher Thich Nhat Hanh writes in his book *Touching Peace*: "In the historical dimension, we have birth certificates and death certificates. . . . This is the world of waves. It is characterized by birth and death, ups and downs, being and non-being. A wave has its beginning and an end, but we cannot ascribe these characteristics to water. In the world of water, there is no birth or death, no being or non-being, no beginning or end." And in his lecture *The Song of No Coming No Going*, he said: "When someone is about to die he may be very afraid. He does not know where he will go. She doesn't know about the reality of no coming no going. He thinks that to be born is, from nothing you become something and to die means from someone, from something you become nothing. So that kind of vacuum that will become makes you very afraid. When you are dying, you think you are becoming nothing, you are going to the unknown. You are very afraid and you are very alone. Even if you are surrounded by many people, you are the only one who is dying. That is why you are lonely and afraid, they go together. There are a few things I would like to say here concerning dying. In fact, people don't die. People do not die when they die, because dying, to us, in our head, dying is: from someone you become no one. You no longer exist. You are caught in the notion of being and non-being. This sheet of paper exists. We are very sure of that because of our idea of existence. We establish the lifetime of the piece of paper. We think that the piece of paper has a beginning and will have an end. But it's very difficult for us to establish the birthdate of the paper. Not only difficult but impossible, because to be born, in our mind is: from nothing you become something, if you already existed before you were born, there's no need of being born. That is what Nagarjuna wrote . . . Before something is born, did it exist or not? If you said, 'It already existed before it was born,' he would laugh and say, 'In that case, what is the use of being born? You are already there.' Looking deeply into this sheet of paper with mindfulness you will see many elements that you would not call paper, like the forest, the forest is in here. Without a forest the trees cannot be, the sheet of paper cannot be, the sunshine, the rain, the minerals, the earth, everything can be found here if we care to look deeply into the sheet of paper. So the sheet of paper, before being perceived as the sheet of paper, had already existed in other forms. Although now it has a new form the content is very much the same—the sunshine, the cloud, the forest are there, very clear, very real. So a birth certificate for this sheet of paper is impossible. This sheet of paper did not come from nothing. We all agree that this has not come from nothing.

For something that has not come from nothing has never been born, and that applies to us. Before we were born we already existed in our mother, and even before we were conceived we were there somehow in our father, in our ancestors. So in fact and according to the teaching of the Buddha we have never been born. When a Zen teacher asks you about your face, your original face before your grandmother was born, he is inviting you to go on a voyage to look for your origin, for your beginning, for your true birthdate, for you to enter into the reality of no birth. If something has never been born, how could that something die? Because to die means, from something you become nothing, nothing at all. Is it possible to reduce something into nothingness? Can you reduce a piece of dust into nothingness? I don't think so. Can you reduce this sheet of paper into nothingness? You cannot. Even if you strike a match and burn this sheet of paper you won't reduce it into nothingness. The sheet of paper will take on other forms. Smoke will come up and become part of a cloud and who knows what it will become tomorrow? It is a very wonderful adventure, going up to the sky and becoming part of a cloud . . . So we look deeply into reality and we are able to see the mystery of no birth and no death, no coming no going. That will relieve us of our fear, our uncertainty. It is impossible for us to say good-bye to someone who is dying, because it is not dying, it is a transformation. We should be very alert, attentive in order to recognize that person now, tomorrow . . . When a cloud is about to be transformed into rain, the cloud will not be scared. It is wonderful to be a cloud floating up there, but it would be also wonderful becoming rain and falling on the ground, on the roof, on the wheat field and supporting life. So being a cloud is wonderful but being rain is also wonderful. Why should that cloud be afraid? But we, we are afraid because we have not been able to see into the true nature of no birth no death, no coming no going. I have proposed to friends that on their birthday instead of singing, 'Happy Birthday to you,' we say, 'Happy Continuation to you.' The song that we sing for the dying is also like that, singing for the continuation in other forms . . . When we observe the waves on the ocean we describe the waves in terms of high, low, small, big, white, not so white, and so on . . . It seems that a wave has birth and then has death. But we know that waves are at the same time water. The waves have to practice in order to see themselves as water. You cannot describe water in terms of waves. You cannot use the adjectives, the nouns, the expressions that you have used to describe waves, because . . . Water belongs to the realm of no birth no death, no high no low, no big no small. The notions, the concepts, the words that we use to describe the waves cannot be used in describing water. The only thing is for waves to look deeply into themselves and see themselves as water. Once waves recognize themselves as water they transcend the fear of birth and death. Because the water is not affected by birth and death, rise and fall."

I know Thich Nhat Hanh's lecture almost by heart, and when I lay on the bench on Smuts Boulevard I thought about my grandfather's father, whom I never saw but whom I resemble quite a bit, according to the pictures, the same as my grandfather, his son, my daughter, and who knows how many others in the coming generations, some of whom will perhaps read these words, which are written for them. It's possible that the grandfather of a reader of this book is yet unborn, I said to myself. Again and again, for the sake of inner peace, or like a lullaby a man sings to himself, I said the words *a cloud cannot die*, which were written by the great teacher, whose life was a treatise on suffering and who saw his country Vietnam destroyed in a senseless offensive not many years following the Second World War, after which, many thought, there would never be another. *A cloud cannot die*, I said to the boulevard's trees, and it's impossible to transform something into nothing, not even a piece of paper, not even this book, which will be called *Netanya*, not even a dust mite, not even a fountain pen, not even this simple bench that's stood on Smuts for fifty years now, which from time to time they paint and then affix with a "wet paint" sign. The pen dried up and the pen will be filled again with fresh ink and will write again as if the intervening years hadn't passed. *A cloud cannot die*, I said to the handful of clouds that hovered in the firmament at four in the morning. It's only possible to change the form of things, and this happens regardless from moment to moment. From this perspective, there is no fundamental difference between what we call life and what we call death. Sometimes I dream about landscapes I've never visited, landscapes of small towns and white poplars. Where did these dreams come from, where did the white flowers come from, I leave this for others to speculate on. I remember frost on windows I never opened. The idea that so many people accept, that out of all the things in the world, only that process called the human spirit, and that alone, can become extinct, is so baseless that there's no point getting hung up on it. This is analogous to arguing that everything can become extinct except the pit of an avocado. I am collaborating on this book with a man who was apparently murdered in the year 1941 in a wave, one of many, of mass extinctions that the world has known, most of them brought on by nature and a minority of them by human beings. This book is written by a living man with the help of many dead, and this proclamation is perfectly obvious, I think, and not the least bit mystical. I chop a carrot with the help of thousands of human beings, I chew leaves of lettuce with the help of thousands of people, some of whom even resemble me. My parents were never interested in literature, whereas I am engrossed in it. There is no doubt that someone or something in the past caused this. Someone in my past opened books and today I open other books, perhaps the very same books, who knows. I think their thoughts, I continue their thoughts, picking up from where they stopped or from another place entirely. I put down my pen at my desk while I was writing and bent over to pet Bob the guinea pig, who was about half a year old, and it seemed as if the father of my grandfather, Shlomo, was petting the guinea pig. Further back than that, I thought and opened my eyes, it's very difficult to see.

The moon came out again from behind a cloud and then I recalled what the astronomy teacher had said many years ago: when you see the moon, you're seeing the sun. One's light is the other's light. We say "moon," but actually it should be "sun-moon." I looked at the moon and saw the sun in the middle of the night. In a recorded lecture I once heard, Thich Nhat Hanh said something like: The sun is my heart. Should it stop beating, should it expire, I would stop beating, I would expire. He said, "I would expire," and at the same moment, all at once, I said, "I would expire," and the two of us thought about the sun, about the very same sun. The heart in the chest is but one of our hearts, he said, pointing at the sun, and I also pointed at the sun, which was now disguised in the light of the moon above my bench. At night there is land and ocean between you and the sun. The moon is also a heart. And all its craters are chambers. There is nothing that is not our heart. All things are hearts, some of them are very obvious, like a bleeding heart, and some are not so obvious, like the sun and the moon, and some of them are distant and concealed, hearts that we don't even know exist. *There is a place that you've never seen and will never visit, and your heart is there.* And you are someone else's heart, a heart for many. Suddenly the writing of literature became clear to me. The guinea pig scurried under the bench on the boulevard as if hiding from the moonlight. A small bird cleaned its feathers incessantly in the tree above me. This tree waits each year for a wind to come and help it shed all its dry leaves. And in the end they fall, all of them, and cover the bench and whoever is lying on it. The bench advanced a bit northward and it was possible to see, in the space between the backrest's brown boards, the gates of the large synagogue and the Chanukah menorah on its roof, which was lit now, at the end of the summer, due to a mishap, four months before the holiday. Someone dragged his feet by the new obituary notices. Below the names the smell of yellow glue was dissipating. In another two or three hours, I knew, the sun would rise between the branches of the menorah, illuminating both the notices and myself.

. . .

In the basement of our hotel there was a tiny belt factory. In order to check the strength of the belts and stretch them, the two belt manufacturers would whip them forcefully against some tables. And sometimes the odor of leather and glue coming from down there would smell so bad that all the hotel guests would escape up to the roof, and my grandfather would stick a clothespin on the end of his nose. "The belts!" he would say nasally, "they're beating the belts!" Below, the whipping continued. Assiduously. Forcefully. Mercilessly. With metal buckles. With thick straps. The tables gritted their teeth with each whipping and kept quiet, but their eyelashes flecked with tears of pain.

. . .

Our guinea pig has a board. He gnaws on it every day, diligently. I heard about a writer who had a similar board, and between each sentence he would dig his teeth into it—his strong, false, golden teeth.

Far down the corridor of memories, door after door is pulled open, heavy curtains are drawn aside, and, as in a rug store, rugs are spread out on the floor one atop another and rugs are hung here and there like partitions, and rugs and carpets are on all the walls; and the windows too, in that corridor, if there are any, are covered, covered in rugs; thick purples and interwoven deep blues and zigzagging, star-studded yellows, thick rugs, rolled-up rugs, a long, thin rug spread out under your feet, "wall to wall," the salesman whispers to him, "wall to wall to wall to wall to wall." And he walks in the soft slippers they gave him inside the store so he wouldn't stain the merchandise, and he forgets what he wanted to buy—just a regular rug. "I'm sure the gentleman will manage here on his own . . . if he gets lost, ring this bell, just lift your hand and ring . . ." and the customer continues wandering through the showrooms, and he whistles in order to hear himself but there's no echo in these padded spaces, and he screams so they'll answer him but his voice is immediately smothered, absorbed like silent steps in a corridor full of sleep, layer upon layer of thick, murmuring carpets. And with the tips of his fingers he removes a bath rug, hanging from a hook, which looks light to him, but its weight is like metal, and behind it a room appears. He rings the bell.

. . .

It was a long, narrow room, actually a closed-in porch. In it were a bookshelf, a single bed, and a sort of very small writing table that was apparently a leftover from childhood. Oh, the poems that we wrote during childhood. At small tables. With pencils that they sharpened for us and which never broke. An adult could have only used such a table with difficulty. In my memory, the room was always dim, submerged. It faced east, toward the carpentry shed and the orange tree, and it had one window with closed wooden shutters. Light reached it in the morning, but by noon it was already dusk there, and afterward evening fell, and by four, darkness had prevailed, night had fallen. Through the closed shutters it was possible to see the yard, beyond which, they told us, was Levy's barbershop in Founders Square. We failed to understand how the places were connected, but we heard the sharpening of the razor and smelled the fragrances. On the outside windowsill, I remember, stood an almost empty jar of honey, through the remains of which two or three bees ate their way. The room never changed, it seemed; the bed was made, with a yellowish cover on it, and on the bookshelf was a row of books published by the People's Library. To this very day, whenever I imagine a workroom fit for a writer, I think about that room: very clean, small, illuminated by a weak light, and in it there's a bed—a bed that always appears a bit swollen, as if declaring its softness—and a small shelf with books on it, no more than twenty, and all of them from the People's Library. A similar room appears in the photograph on the cover of Yuval Shimoni's novel *A Room*, which was indeed published by the People's Library. A table, a chair, you sit at the table and look silently at your empty lined notebook, your fountain pen, the fossil you place on every table, a small ancient animal, with wings and a beak, an ancient, prehistoric songbird. And after a few hours, half a page is already filled with words and you lie down on the bed and nap and dream the rest of the story. Once my father and grandfather went up to fix something on one of the top floors of the hotel, and I remained in the guesthouse below. I entered that room, which was always distinct and separate from the other rooms of the house, like those rooms that get reconstructed inside museums, which you're not supposed to enter, but rather just look at, as if they were framed pictures. It was a hot morning then, and light broke through the shutters and fell on the bed. I climbed onto that same soft hill on the bed and immediately fell asleep. I dreamed that my grandmother was standing there saying to me, "Get up, get up, you're not allowed to sleep here." In another few weeks I will be forty years old. That is to say, I have so far spent ten years asleep. Perhaps fifteen. When I woke up, my grandmother stood on the thick carpet spread out there, half of it under the bed and half of it reaching almost to the bookshelf's wall. She covered my forehead with damp wool. I rose slowly and went into the kitchen with eyelids stuck together. The wool was still up against my forehead, and I looked for the bathroom sink in order to rinse my face. To my amazement, everyone was sitting there: my parents, my grandfather and grandmother, and Dr. Kugelman as well, the doctor who lived on the ground floor of our house on Bialik Street, who I found out had been called. The wool fell to my feet. They looked at me, shocked by what they saw, and I stepped into the crooked circle that they made with their chairs and exited it and went up to the sink and rinsed my face and head in warm water. A sleepwalker can walk on air for a few steps and not fall, even if there's an abyss below. My grandfather smoked, put his hand outside the kitchen window, and blew his smoke out there. The smoke returned home via the bathroom window and hit me in the nose when I went to pee. I barely noticed all this, and only wanted to go back to sleep. When they saw that I was turning to go back to the room, they blocked my path. My mother lifted up a bucket. Something was written on it. She was about to spill all the water on my head in order to wake me up. Ice water in a tin bucket. With eyelids slightly less stuck together, I retreated to the refrigerator opposite the door, to get a little water or seltzer to drink. I opened the door of the refrigerator with some difficulty, like a person pulling open a heavy gate, as in a castle. There was a sort of vacuum in there, the refrigerator was pulling the door from the inside, it was as though there were someone strong inside, waiting in the cold, whose job this was. I struggled with the refrigerator until I vanquished it with a cry, and I opened the door. A large carp split in two crosswise was on the nearest shelf. A thin layer of frost covered its eyes and teeth. Its tail, I noticed in terror, had fallen down below a few levels, to the vegetable shelf. It turned out I had been asleep twenty-four hours, and no one could wake me.

. . .

I feel that the end of these sketches is approaching. I am sitting on the guinea pig's footstool on a hot evening, the twentieth of August. I brought a fan out to the porch in order to make it easier on the two of us and indeed it appears that he enjoys the light breeze. He stretches himself out to be petted. The things I say to him I do not write down in this notebook. I think he understands my speech, although perhaps not all the subtleties. But who understands all the subtleties? I certainly don't. I looked at myself in the mirror today after my shower and identified a reddish hue in my wet hair. My brother is a redhead, as are a couple of other family members as well. Where did this color in our hair come from? Hundreds of years are buried inside this hair. And the north. And the cold. There are red hairs in Bob the guinea pig's fur as well, and in the wind the fan blows on us, both his hair and my hair flutter a bit. I want to cry but there are other people in the apartment, so I put down my pen and close the notebook. Using a teaspoon, I pick up the droppings Bob leaves behind, check to see that he has enough drinking water for the night hours gradually falling. Outside, on the street, on my bench on the boulevard, sitting close together, shoulder to shoulder, are my grandfather and his father smoking a single cigarette that they pass to each other every few puffs.

. . .

When they dug the foundations of the Park Hotel, they found the remains of an ancient dolphin in a beach cliff, and we went to see it with a few thousand other Netanyans. My grandfather pushed his way into the inner circle, carrying me on his shoulders. He let me hold his red health credentials and leaned over the skeleton while I was still on his shoulders. He said to my father, “Each one had a short whistle that was specific to him only. A rising sound—a descending sound. The sound was in fact his name. Thus did each dolphin say to the rest of the members of his school: I exist.” As he said this, he lowered his head, brought his lips close to the dolphin’s skull, half-buried in limestone, and whistled a short whistle. A short rising sound, a short descending sound. I held tight to his thinning hair so I wouldn’t fall. A whistle came back like an echo from within the hole, a bit different and fainter than his own.

. . .

I saw him sitting at a table in a café on Herzl Street with my astronomy teacher. A round star map was spread out on the table in front of them, and from a distance I also saw that this was not the usual map. This was, without a doubt, a different sky. Shaken, I knew I was dreaming. I raised my eyes to the sky above the sky on the round map. A map atop a map, I thought, in those words exactly. Other stars glittered there in the light of Café Whitman, at the foot of the Hotel Tel Aviv. I took a step or two forward.

The two of them were so immersed in the map, and the café was so busy, that they didn't notice me even when I was standing right next to them, just an arm's length away. Two servings of ice cream were melting slowly in their bowls. Every few moments my grandfather and the astronomy teacher moved a bit around the table, in order to compensate for the Earth's rotation. I sat down on a vacant stool between them, and they still didn't notice me, or they didn't care. They didn't say a thing, not even when I rested my cheek on the map, which was soft as new carpeting or the fur of an animal that had just been brushed. Despite my position, I saw the names of stars and constellations, but ones I'd never heard about before, strange names from myths I hadn't learned. Lupus next to Centaurus! A Telescope and a Triangle! Could it be? Now I understood that this was a map of the sky in the southern hemisphere, to which my grandfather was soon to sail as part of that same cruise around Africa for senior citizens, and that I was witnessing a private lesson about the southern stars. Four or five other travelers, laden with backpacks and sleeping bags, ice cream cones in their hands, on their way to the small port of Netanya, were waiting in line for instructions too. One of those waiting said, "I once tried to navigate around Patagonia with a northern star map. In the end I arrived at what I thought was Antarctica, but I was mistaken, it was the North Pole. Well, the snow wasn't so different." And another traveler said to him, "Cold is cold," and then added, as she faced all of us, "if you had eyes that could see gamma rays and you were in the southern hemisphere, every night you would see a large, bright ring glowing in the sky." All of us raised our heads, including my grandfather and the teacher, even though we weren't in the southern hemisphere but instead in Netanya, and even though none of us could see gamma rays with our naked eyes, except for my grandfather. And because I had fixed my gaze for some time on the map of the southern sky, whose stars were glittering points of phosphorus, it seemed to me that the southern stars were dotting Netanya's own heavenly dome. Argo Navis, Crux! I called out the names of the constellations, which glowed in print on the clouds over my head. I must be off, said my grandfather to the travelers. I must take my place on deck. Rest my head on rolled-up rope soaked in seawater. See the wide-open sea in every direction. Wake up at four in the morning and go out to the stern wrapped up in a blanket. Scrub the boards of the deck using a brush with no handle. Sleep above the water wide and deep that begins right below your bunk. Huddle inside my bunk. Sing a shanty. Lean against dirty, foul-smelling barrels. Touch the anchor's ancient iron. Disembark at one port and then another. Cry in a disgusting bar in a distant harbor that reminds everyone of home.

He fell silent. The ice cream had become a puddle of vanilla and banana. The teacher folded up the map but stopped when he got to my head, which was still resting on its edge. From out of the folds rose the dawn like an old man walking up a flight of stairs. In the nearby train station, Netanya Central, in Independence Square, swarthy, bespectacled porters were already waiting next to carriages whose horses were standing and dozing, waiting for the first people to depart for the port at Siren Beach—there they would get on the ship that would take them on what for them would be a simple adventure, but for the porters would be a return after being away for a very long time.

. . .

The police searched day and night for the kidnapper. The boy Shimon Oded had been compelled by his abductor to call his parents from a public telephone in order to prove that he was still alive, and he'd said to them, in order to prove that he was indeed the child in question, "I had a hamster." He clearly said *I had* a hamster, in past tense, and my father heard the radio broadcast and said, "That boy will not be coming back." On the same day, the Park Hotel, located at the end of Bialik Street, went up in flames. At first no one noticed. Soon after, my mother said, "Something's burning," and went over to the heater. A few minutes later, the neighbors' heads appeared in their windows, and they wiggled their noses with emphasis as if to pantomime the act of sniffing. After this, coughs were heard from the end of the street. All of Bialik Street filled up with black smoke, as though from an exhaust pipe. A wind came from the sea and carried the smoke down the street, and the street was like those rivers that overflow their banks and flood houses up to the second story. You could have opened an upstairs window to jump into the stifling river or lower in a boat. Dr. Kugelman came out of his apartment on the ground floor, his stethoscope in his ears and a needle held out as if he were going to give the smoke a shot. Women in white masks burst out of beauty parlors flustered and groping, slices of cucumber over their eyes. And Fabian Zachariah, who had come home for a short visit, while the boy was still missing, descended from the fifth floor, drawings and paintings in hand to be saved from the approaching fire. Paddling in the smoke, we rowed upriver to the hotel, into the westerly wind, following the fire trucks that had arrived in the meantime and cut off the street lengthwise. The sounds of sirens echoed in the smoke and Zachariah's paintbrushes whipped around. The former mayor, who lived in a villa right across from our house, crawled by in a private car, dressed in a suit, to take in the sight, clearing a path through the crowd, slowly cutting across the thirty-five meters to the fire. He waved weakly to his subjects crowding the corner of Bialik Street and Hamatmid Street, totally protected, digesting as usual a lovely breakfast, surrounded by two or three comets at a distance. The fire had already reached the fourth floor, where it raged and consumed curtains and beds recently cleaned and made up by the hotel's housekeeping staff. The beds called out to the fire and the fire rested its head on the pillows, on the feathers. Chickens erupted from the kitchen, escaped under the aegis of the tumult, fled to the sea. The top half of the Park Hotel was still a hotel, and theoretically it was still possible to sleep in it, to stand on a balcony facing the Mediterranean Sea and watch sailors over breakfast: butter opposite sails. But the bottom half of the building had already been devoured by fire. The mayor opened his car window a bit and the voice of the kidnapped boy, which had been heard many times that same morning, emerged from his radio, saying, "I had a hamster," "I had a hamster," and was then swallowed up by the smoke. The window closed immediately. I stood there terrified and watched the western end of street burn. Our Belgian neighbor, who would give me his stamps and would fill up a bath for this purpose and have all his envelopes float in it so he could remove the wet stamps from them and dry them on his soap dish, lit a high-quality Belgian cigarette, broke a bar of chocolate over his bent knee, and said, "In Antwerp there's a fire like this every day, no reason to get excited. Fire also needs to eat, from time to time, you know." I stood there and thought about *our* hotel, Hotel Tel Aviv, which wasn't far from there. It was revealed to me then for what it was: so small, only three stories high; not the place for a great many suntanned guests and tourists in bathing suits; never serving rich breakfasts of warm bread and squares of butter and spreads in every color of the rainbow, as well as fresh-squeezed juices; empty of pure white linens, stretched tight over large beds—no, instead, it was a near ruin, a sinking building full of junk and stones and wood and metal that for me were nothing but parts of a story, nothing but memories that mostly weren't even my memories but rather father and grandfather's memories. And I thought for a moment that if I set it on fire, all these people and all these photographers would show up there too, and would watch it and remember it. And the mayor would come running and fall on the flames.

Not far from there, Zachariah our neighbor, whose beard was getting rather long, sat on the roof of a car in order to see better, and with a few powerful brushstrokes feverishly painted on a hastily stretched canvas the hotel and the fire and the masses that had congregated at the west end of Bialik. He painted the firemen stretching their life nets open, the first jumpers from the top floors, fat naked women still adorned with suds from their interrupted baths, bespectacled men with *tallit* bags in their gentle hands, armed police in uniform and hotel workers in scorched red formalwear. And one soldier jumped as well. One after another they jumped down and presented their images to the entire city, becoming a photograph in some newspaper or history whose caption, as it were, could be: "The Early Eighties: I stand in the air for a moment and at my back a burning building and a sea." He painted the flames reflected in the waves and the panic of the tourists whose vacation had gone up in flames and the light of the sun that poured into the blaze. And then he jerked his head toward me and painted me too. The city sat idly by, everyone wanted to see the fire, it was like an execution in the central square. For years there hadn't been a fire like this in the city, a pillar of fire as in the Bible, and more than that, right on the seashore. Photographers photographed until their film ran out and the fire was contained and forced down to the first story, like a damaged elevator being arduously lowered floor by floor. From out of the strangled, grumbling fire rose the remains of the hotel, the king of the sea whose form had changed into a heap of ash, wrapped in a long mantle of damp soot and smoke, only its head still young and healthy. Another wind came and scattered the smoke as well as most of the people who'd been coughing, and they, like butterfly hunters without nets, gave chase to their coughs, fleeing eastward. Our neighbor from the fifth floor displayed his magnificent, still-wet painting for all to see, and the Belgian neighbor considered it with one eye shut, like an expert, chewing away. The hotel-on-fire performance was about to come to an end (and not far from there stood our hotel, the Hotel Tel Aviv, without fire and without smoke and, to tell the truth, without guests either). The insurance appraisers were about to head out, brushing up on the appropriate regulations and fixing their ties as they considered the full meaning of the word "arson" and its unlimited implications for insurance purposes, while kissing, excitedly, their beautiful, so very young, and thoroughly insured wives. We were about to return home and to the remainder of our much less interesting day, to homework on ancient Greece, when from the other end of the street a not-unfamiliar voice was heard. We turned our heads and saw my grandfather, barefoot, pajamas over his skin, smoke over his head, and a tin bucket filled halfway with water in his hand. He ran toward us, panting. "They announced that there's a fire on the twelve o'clock news," he said.

. . .

Silent, plain-clothed policemen filled Bialik Street during those weeks. The ring of pursuit grew tighter and tighter. On behalf of the police, strange children penetrated our groups as we played games in the courtyard, asking questions as though making innocent conversation. At night steps were heard on the roof. You would leave your home and someone would remove his ear from an adjacent door and escape down the stairs. There were private investigators as well, an entire agency, actually, eight or nine remarkably similar detectives, just like brothers. We would run into them in the garbage room, right up against the wall: there they were, disguised as trash cans. We would apologize for disturbing them and they would move a bit and let us toss out our garbage. Afterward, they would inspect all the refuse. We asked if we were suspects and they said, "Absolutely."

. . .

Behind the garbage room, in a corner of the rear courtyard, there was a tree, and one day a house of sorts appeared in its branches. Who built it for us, we didn't know. Though perhaps the house was really just a few boards. And a ladder as well: a few more boards nailed to the tree trunk. And once a window opened in the apartment building and a head came out to call the painter's son, who was at the very top of the tree. He didn't answer. So his mother came down and stood at the foot of the tree. One of his shoes peeked out from among the tall branches. A brown orthopedic shoe, a heavy shoe of hard leather with a metal sole and a shoelace like twisted rope, tied tight. It was a bright winter day. They thought that he'd fallen asleep. So they sent me up to get him. We were good friends. I climbed the ladder, placed a foot on the "roof" of the wooden house, and climbed to the upper branches, where he was perched. There I saw him sitting and staring into space. Only then did I notice, from up high, the blue lights of the police. They'd closed off Bialik from every side, and the street was filling up with them, hundreds of police on horses and with their dogs. But the boy hadn't noticed the commotion, apparently. He stared resolutely at the clouds and the cold, charred hotel. I turned my head and saw his father below, surrounded by policemen, being led to a police car. In his desperation, he broke through the ring of police and tried to escape to the garbage room. A policeman hiding there jumped out and captured him immediately. The painter stood there defeated and raised his eyes to the lowest shutters. I looked at his son, but he still didn't seem to have noticed the situation; he was leaning his neck on a branch and looking off into the distance. I reached out to put my hand on his shoulder, but I didn't touch him, I hesitated and then pulled back. Below, the police were taking out handcuffs and clattering their keys. Surrendering, the painter held out his two hands and closed his eyes. But they cuffed his ankles.

. . .

"I had a hamster. Now I'm in a car with dirty windows that are closed. I'm sitting next to the man that caught me and put me in the car. Who is he? Who is he? We're in his car. On the back seat next to me is a *challah* and a balloon. We sleep in the car. He calls someone every few days. From inside the locked car I see him saying things into the payphone. Once I saw the numbers he dialed. It took me a moment to understand: It's our number. Where did he get our number from. I fall asleep and wake up in the car. I dream about a demon. I don't see him, but he's there behind the door. A small line of light. Suddenly he's next to me. He grabs me and lifts me up. I'm heavy for him, he grabs me and lifts me up. As though someone else is fighting to keep me down. He's strong too, whoever it is; he pulls me too, pulls me down. It's like there are strings tied to my ankles. I know, they're fighting against him. But he's stronger. He holds me and he lifts me up. And he holds me and he lifts me up and he lifts me up. And he lifts me up."

. . .

Approximately 540 million years ago they suddenly appear: the trilobites. Creatures with eyes, legs, and hearts. Defenseless. Beautiful as stars. They are the first proof of the existence of life in the ancient past, since they left behind signs, imprinted their existence in stone, like a child carving his name on a tree trunk in the rear courtyard of a house in Netanya: Dror. They had skeletons, therefore they could become fossilized, therefore we can see them. We don't know a thing about life before them. It's possible that there wasn't any life then at all; or else, if there was, it just didn't leave any signs in stone, because, say the authors of *Rare Earth*, it was too soft. I'm partial to the second explanation. We existed—I won't apologize for the use of first person plural—well before the trilobites, and like them we were defenseless. This was at the end of the long ice age, approximately six hundred million years ago. But in contrast to the trilobites, we didn't have eyes and legs. We had a soft, transparent heart wrapped in something we didn't know enough to name. How to describe us? We were sort of transparent strings. Almost puffs of wind. Light, without color, without bones, without the ability to move. We would float on currents. And sometimes there were creatures that fell upon us from their hiding places, baring their teeth. No, they didn't have teeth of course, but today there's no word in the language better than that. And then we were destroyed. For no reason, just for existing, I suppose, and for the things we dared to say. Our enemies emerged again and again. They didn't even want to eat us, we were thin and nearly transparent, after all (though so were they). We crawled under flat stones, we were pushed into narrow spaces. We crawled up onto tables. It's obvious that all of this would have been invisible to the naked eye without a very strong microscope. And, indeed, no one saw it. No one saw it to such an extent that we ourselves weren't sure that it was happening. The hypothesis that it was a bad dream that might still pass grew stronger and stronger. In any case, all this happened inside a drop of water on the end of a sea anemone in the depths of the ocean. But now the anemone is dead, the drop already consumed by the ocean surrounding it hundreds of millions of years, days, hours ago, or else it evaporated in the heat of the sun, which was surely weaker in those days, but its light was enough, even after only a few seconds, to bring about our destruction.

. . .

I don't remember too much of my life as a trilobite in the Cambrian period. Even on the shallow sea floor, the water pressure was unbearable. There were days in which any movement was painful, so we remained mostly stationary. I say "we remained" in first person plural, but it's unclear to me whether I was alone or not. Even moving our eyes—and sure, we had eyes!—no, out of the question. It was quite dark there anyway. And we were quite small. It's possible that I spent some time asleep. During the long nights, I dreamed about an opaque wall. Hundreds of pictures that had been hanging on it were removed one day and white rectangles left behind. The meaning of the dream was hidden from me then.

Today, when I recall those days, half a billion years ago, I remember nothing but the burden of the salty water and the light above the water. But the dream I dreamed then I sometimes dream today as well. The truth of the matter is that I don't understand it any better today. Yesterday I dreamed again: An entrance to a giant apartment. The walls were big. The rectangles marked out all over the walls. But the apartment was flooded with water. An old man struggled with a squeegee.

A few years ago I bought a trilobite fossil from a different species. We can be found by the millions in places where ancient seas dried up. At night the fossil lies behind the transparent partition at my side, and I try to fall asleep, despite his presence. I splashed him with a little seawater. I know that he despises my room, my apartment, the clocks in the apartment, the ticking across from me and over him. So I broke the clocks. In vain. I know that he despises me and is waiting patiently for me to disappear. Once I dreamed—no, this was reality—that I got out of bed and removed all the pictures from my walls. Perhaps he'll finally be reconciled to his new home. I—it can be said—love him. Yet he desires nothing but my extinction.

. . .

From where I was lying on the bench, I saw across the boulevard, at a distance of perhaps ten meters, our old Kia automobile, a '98 model, dirty from the droppings of the boulevard's birds. On the front windshield I saw the university parking stickers that I've affixed to it year after year, layer after layer, for more than ten years now. I looked at the scratches, dents, nicks. The life of the car was written for all to see on that blue tin can at five in the morning—if that was in fact the time. All that I wanted at that moment was to sit down inside the car and start the engine and drive as far away as possible. I looked at the blue car and thought about the continental drift taking place under my bench right then, carrying the bench on a continent's migration of sorts, with mountain ranges for wings, carrying it very slowly to an unknown destination, which we could call—why not?—its nest. When I was a child, I dressed up as a bird and my mother made me a cracked egg from which I hatched, as it were, and the egg was set out in a large nest made of hay. I imagined the books we write as continents drifting or birds that we send out into the world, so that in case of extinction a part of us might still be found far away, which will increase our chances of survival. But the birds fly and fly and the Earth is covered in water. They imagine that there's a white rock somewhere down there but it's nothing more than a wave's foam and they drown. This book is my fossil. I thought, I'll get into the car right now and drive away from this bench and my thoughts. Bench, bench, I whispered to it, you are full of memories; where did they come from? I'll sit myself down in the comfortable seat and turn the key and drive. But to where? If the direction of the moon's rotation were reversed, our gray neighbor would crash into us, someday. But since it moves in the direction of our rotation and accompanies us like a shadow, it actually gets farther from us year after year. I pictured the way I would hold the steering wheel and turn it, and just drive around the neighborhood at first, then leave town, circle the city and the planet, increase my speed a bit more, and finally take off. Neptune also has a moon, Triton, and it rotates in reverse, opposite the rotation of its mother planet. Therefore, someday, it will fall toward her and crash. The blue car stood there. My latest parking sticker, from the year 2009, glowed in the first light, which came not from the sun, but rather from the large synagogue's menorah, which due to a mishap was lit all year long, even on Yom Kippur. Chanukah's eighth candle on Yom Kippur—there were those who saw this as quite ominous. Four hundred million years ago, a year on earth was four hundred days and each day was shorter. Less time for writing, more time for sleeping, I thought and coughed. The cough filled the street, and birds flew out of a nearby tree and then returned and were absorbed into the foliage as they changed their colors like dawn's chameleons. A cough—and then birds; for some reason this alarmed me. Less time for writing, fewer hours of light, a faster rotation and a weak, distant sun. But soon the knowledge that I too had been then filled me with calm. Everything had always been. The birds again rose up from the leaves, and another cough exploded out of me. Though it wasn't properly a cough, to tell you the truth. It was a song. It was a very beautiful song, one only I heard.

. . .

My memories, plankton in a strong current, are swept along to kindergarten, and its gravity, with the teacher at its center, like a massive, extinguished sun, pulls them down, down to the seesaws and sandboxes. And they're growing too, the memories, from moment to moment. You move your fins a bit so you won't crash, but it's in vain. You're sucked into a small chair, a stool of sorts, and the teacher, whose name is Yaffa (yesterday my father said to me: "Yaffa? The teacher? Of course she's still alive, what kind of question is that? Why, she's still quite young. I saw her last week by the movie theater"), in a silence that your crashing somehow didn't disturb, says: The Holocaust survivors didn't disappear. They're here with us, in this kindergarten. Do you see them, dear children? And indeed you notice them suddenly, how well they were camouflaged, such colors they've developed, they're there next to the box of silkworms, or they're standing in the kitchenette eating sandwiches the children gave them, and sometimes stealing from their backpacks. Our kindergarten was, and still is a close neighbor of the great synagogue. A few days ago I went to photograph it, but when I arrived I discovered it had been destroyed. I stood with my camera ready and nothing was there. Only the red, metal gate remained, facing nothing, and a few childish words on a low wall. I stood there. I read from the wall.

I remember the silkworms that were in the kindergarten and the swing sets in the courtyard, one of which I fell from when I saw a Holocaust survivor holding onto the bars of the kindergarten fence and watching us play. He was a relative of the teacher, and she invited him each and every year to tell us about his suffering. I wanted to hug him, but how do you hug a person like that, broken and tortured? *I have a nail*, he said, I have a nail in my head. Our caterpillars waited in their cocoons. We had ceremonies, we would prepare giant letters covered in silver paper and gold paper and attach them to poles. We would stand in order and from out of the jumble a glowing word would rise to be revealed before everyone's eyes. IDF. Netanya. Jerusalem. The Name of God. Peace. Remember. In kindergarten we learned to love the army, peace, and Jerusalem. Like a writer without a pen, Yaffa would say: Ephraim, Adi, Dror, and Emil—to the right. And a word would appear. And four more girls, Tamar, Yael, Hagit, and

Atalia, by the corner with the guinea pigs—and another word has already been written. And sometimes: Adi, stand next to Tamar, and Yael—to the right of Dror; and already a big change, a revision, that we, the children, never once guessed. We revised and rewrote from behind our big letters. And think of the kids who got to be a special end-of-word letter! And especially a final *M—mem*: ם—which is a window you look through but through which you're also seen, like the portrait of a prince in a gold frame. *Challahs* were sliced, balloons were blown up, and from the window at the end of our holy capital city I saw my parents and my grandfather and my grandmother and next to them our French aunt (who arrived "for only a short weekends, don't make no anything, I sleep in bathtub like always *mon chéri*, I brought food in the iceberg"), who at first didn't notice me at all behind my letter. But then my mother saw me and said to them, he's there, behind the *mem*. Only then did I see that my uncle was standing next to them and in his hand was the old camera I would eventually take with me to London and forget in some park on a bench, a roll of exposed film inside it. I want to remember him like that, looking at me a few months before he was killed. Only I can't help but remember the lens of the camera, instead, and the light of the flash, sending a strong, sudden glare to the golden frame of my final letter, closing the eyes of all the children and then the eyes of their parents facing them as well, burning the overly sensitive film and going up in flames over the blocks of basalt and thorns and then disappearing.

. . .

I had an aunt who married a Cro-Magnon. An ancient variety of *Homo sapiens*, but in a suit and tie he almost resembled us. Short, muscular, and quick. Were it not for his habit of biting into any bits of nearby wood, it would have been possible to mistake him for a modern. It was he who made the Lascaux paintings, he claimed, even though he refused to return to his achievement, saying that he had no intention of sneaking into the cave, now that it was all closed off, and as to the option of recreating his opus on canvas, well, that would be pathetic, as he said.

They lived in Paris, and he was a quite well-known attorney for a giant communications company. His employers knew nothing about his past. Yes, there was certainly something strange about him, but they dismissed this as being part of his Jewishness. "And so ugly," they whispered. But there were a few other women—of which my aunt knew nothing, apparently.

Because of her husband's origins, my aunt went to study paleontology at the Sorbonne with Griffault. She began as a hobbyist, but quite quickly transferred to the PhD program and even earned herself a position. Dug into some glaciers. Her husband was, as usual, late to the graduation ceremony. Came in five minutes before the end, peeking at his watch all the while. Griffault furrowed his brow.

"When he dies," my aunt said to me once, in her usual strange mixture of Yiddish and French, "I will bury him and wait. Trink a *bisl* tea, *mon petit*. And then, a few years later, I will dig him up," she said. "I will dig him up alone. And what will be found there, to great surprise, will bring me world renown."

. . .

Someone dragged an abandoned refrigerator along the asphalt at the head of Dizengoff Street just before dawn. Dragged dragged and stopped. Dragged dragged and stopped. My grandfather said: "There you have it, the creation of the world."

The demolition order from the city of Netanya hit the seventy-year-old mailbox at 25 Dizengoff, making a knocking sound. Like flies on the rim of a rusty trashcan. You have a month to vacate the hotel. Make way for the bulldozer. In the small room facing the courtyard, my grandfather sat on the single bed, opposite the small shelf filled with books published by the People's Library. When I entered the room I again saw the bronze memorial plaque that he'd received from the armored corps. Some dust had stuck to its felt lining. The unit's emblems and ranks and sundry decorations were all covered with a thick, chalky dust and lint, to the point that in the dim light of the room the plaque looked like a stone. Medications were piled up in a cooking pan. My grandfather sat on the bed and an old issue of the *Davar* daily newspaper was spread out on his knees. This, he said, is the issue from the day your father was born. He would keep the issues from important dates, in order to be reminded of what had been going on then. 2,500 tons of bombs were dropped on Berlin when your father was born, on February 17, 1944, a date that is, by the way, also the birthdate of the great basketball player Miki Berkovich, an entirely random fact that has been recalled proudly hundreds of times in our family. Fifteen thousand were murdered in prisoner of war camps, said a smaller headline on the front page. My father was born on this day. You might consider this newspaper his first diaper. You are diapered in this, you entered into this on day one. It was hot and stifling. The hotel, whose greatness had already been diminished, seemed to sink into the earth and so become shorter. It was February '99, if I'm not mistaken. Two hundred and fifty million years ago, my grandfather said to me, or I said to him, following a reading of the final, hair-raising chapters of Peter Ward's book *Gorgon*, a severe extinction consumed the Earth. Ward is of the opinion that the reason for this was a combination of a drop in the percentage of oxygen in the atmosphere along with a concurrent increase in the percentage of carbon dioxide, and on the heels of this an increase of six degrees Celsius in the average global temperature. *Gorgon* describes a research trip in the Karoo desert in South Africa. The trip lasted a dozen years, but I only gave my grandfather Ward's conclusions: After the great extinction, which ended what we call the Permian period and the entire Paleozoic era, came the Mesozoic era, and with it the Triassic and the Jurassic, and the rocks from the Triassic until the middle of the Jurassic, over the course of approximately fifty million years, are different from the rocks of the Permian, in that they are red. When Ward saw this, he understood that the color came from the oxygen, which had sunk into the earth when it disappeared from the air. Imagine the ground rusting out under your feet as you struggle for every breath. At the end of the Permian, the percentage of oxygen in the air dropped to about half of its level today, and the extinction of numerous species became unavoidable. The Lystrosaurus didn't go extinct, since it could still breathe thanks to its large lungs, which perhaps evolved during times of low oxygen, or in high mountains; when the percentages of oxygen fell, they migrated to sea level and continued to breathe as they had before, while around them all the other animals suffocated. A Lystosaurus skeleton's enormous ribcage testifies to the large lungs the creatures must have had. Do you hear, Grandfather? He said, "Yes, what did you say? They breathed?" And tapped on the newspaper and said, for a moment I forgot what my name is. I woke up today, here, in this bed. You know that it's forbidden for anyone to sleep here. But I was walking in my sleep and apparently I fell. Don't know why. In fact, it wasn't the first time. When I woke up I'd forgotten my name. I tried to think of it, I tossed names to myself, out loud. I searched for something that would remind me, I grabbed this newspaper, I thought something in the paper would remind me of my name, but it didn't work. I said to him, "It happens, it's like a person sometimes forgetting his telephone number." He said, "I disconnected the telephone, I no longer want calls. You know, I get phoned by all sorts of, c'mon, you know, what are they called?" and then he added, who would have believed that we'd get to the year 2000? I'm thinking about traveling to Africa. There's a cruise for the elderly, look, everything's written in the paper, and he pointed first at the 1944 newspaper and then, when he noticed his mistake, at another newspaper, fresh, which had been tossed to the floor. Heat and asphyxiation, I said to him, but a cough drowned out my words. I said again, Heat and asphyxiation annihilated them a quarter billion years ago. But the Lystrosaurus survived, do you hear, Grandfather? Apparently it had particularly large lungs. It was the only animal from among the mammal-like reptiles that made it through the asphyxiation, apparently because at first it evolved in a very high place, with limited oxygen. Its breathing apparatus had been prepared in advance. Birds too fly over Mt. Everest, where we would suffocate, because they have a type of respiratory system that makes it possible for them to fly and breathe at high altitudes. "Elephants know how to fly, too," replied my grandfather, grumbling, and what could I say to that. I asked him, "And afterward, did you remember your name?" But he answered, "Elephants too, elephants too," and then said, still looking at the 1944 newspaper, in almost total darkness, "You know, bird lungs and dinosaur lungs, it's the same lungs. Basically, a bird is a small dinosaur." And what could I say to that? "It's 'Zvi,' you know," I said to him, concerned, and he said, "C'mon now, 'Zvi'?

Now you tell me? But I had another name once. My father pulled down my sock at the station. Of course you never met him, that was before your time. I was almost late for the train." There is, it seems, a sort of life force, and it always burst back out whenever possible, when the conditions are ripe, he said, and then fell to the bed tired and crushed the old newspaper with his body. I'm tired, reading the newspaper in the dark, it really exhausts you. All the words and the bombs. The telephones that ring at night for you and scare you and no one's there, and you scream to nobody but yourself, Hello, hello. I took a few steps in order to read the headline of the newspaper of the day my father was born, most of which was crushed under my grandfather's body, and then I brushed against something that was attached to the leg of the bed and I dropped down onto the mattress next to him. "Two hundred and fifty million years, you said?" he asked. I remembered then that this whole time a copy of the demolition order from Netanya's city engineer had been in my pocket; I'd been sent over to bring it to him. They'd passed a municipal bylaw especially for our hotel. The room's small window was closed, but the roof of the hotel—which had collapsed some time ago—was open and we could have seen the color of the sky, had we only opened our eyes. "It's a shame I didn't meet your father," I said to him, and he said, "There was some story then . . . with a rhinoceros . . . I no longer recall the details . . . but you were there, no? No? Nonsense, you saw it come, and he almost crushed you. I remember. They pulled you back by your belt." I don't remember when we fell asleep on that bed, or when we woke up. You sleep beside another person and his dream always becomes your dream. From his sleep he speaks all your hidden thoughts. When he jumps in fear you jump with him. But my grandfather and me, no. We just dozed for an hour. And next to us the two newspapers also dozed, breathed, rustled softly. I dreamed that I entered a giant house, and newspapers were stuck to the walls like wallpaper, and I went up close to read what was written but I reached an open window, I knew it would be better if I didn't read the paper, so I looked through the window and there was a tree, standing in a light rain, so beautifully lit, and next to it the end of a faucet, with chrysanthemums sticking out from inside it. Suddenly I was next to the tree, I was crying for joy in my dream. I circled the tree, and then I saw that newspaper was stuck to it as well. "The glue is alive," I heard someone say to me, "your fingers are in danger." But I circled the tree again, it was no longer clear which side I was on, but I saw that the flowers were still there. And then I saw that I too was there. I see myself there.

I put the demolition order in the pan. I got up and crossed for the last time, my grandfather and grandmother's apartment in the hotel, from which all of the furniture had been removed, save for a few last pieces. I approached the refrigerator, which was no longer there, and I opened the door easily and a cold light washed over me. I entered the refrigerator; I leaned against its wall. I closed the door and the light went out immediately. Above, in the hotel, in all the abandoned rooms, more and more doves gathered, huddling into their feathers, dozing on broken cornices; on collapsing windows; on beautiful, destroyed chairs from Warsaw; and inside clocks that in their youth crossed wide seas for days, a big hand pointing at the moon and a small hand pointing out to the water; dozing on hangers that had seen the palace windows of Krakow more than a hundred years ago, when they passed through the main streets in an open carriage, hanging, rattling, lightweight, and joyous after all the jackets had been removed from them and passed around, so that people could be wrapped up in them during the coming winter, in the snow that would without a doubt fall this year as well.

. . .

Father's birthday falls on the same day that the legendary basketball player Miki Berkovich was born. We bring this up every time that we celebrate my dad's birthday. At birthday parties we watch selected clips from Miki Berkovich's big games, always the same clips, and afterward lift Father up on a chair, actually a sort of small wooden stool that he's been dragging with him from year to year since childhood. And once, when father—and Miki Berkovich too!—was sixty, we bought him a basketball as a present. On his birthday our father often said to us: "While we get older and older, Miki Berkovich always makes a basket. Without the help of the backboard. From so very far away. So it is, year after year. He never ever misses."

. . .

Chet Raymo, in his book *The Soul of the Night*, describes it. A rather grim picture. It's the universe after every one of its lights has gone out. All the other suns stop burning and die. One final sun is flickering. Last rays. The light scatters and fades. Darkness descends, a night that won't soon end. This isn't a temporary solar eclipse. This isn't a long winter. This is night for billions of years. Perhaps for eternity. The sun, all the suns, the framework of the sky, the galaxies, still travel their paths. Only they're extinguished now, dark. Total darkness. Total night. Sunrises and sunsets of darkness upon darkness. There is still gravity, there is still motion, but there is no light. Waiting for the universe to finally collapse in upon itself so that everything will start over from the beginning. It's reasonable to assume that this will happen, but it won't happen in another hour, and it won't happen tomorrow. In the meantime, the cold planets spin in dark silence. Luckily, there's no one looking at them. All eyes are shut.

. . .

My grandfather rose from the bed in a jerk, struck the newspapers as if searching for something, noticed that I was still there, asked me, very scared, truly terrified, "Who's our mayor now in Netanya? What? *Who is the mayor?*" And a few days before he passed away, he told me that he'd been informed he had been nominated for president.

. . .

Twenty years after the Yom Kippur War, he would still dream that dream. He's in the airport with his three sons. In England. They arrive at the airport and begin walking through the corridors. His passport was cut, canceled, and he knows that the moment has come for him to provide some explanation for this. And he knows that it's possible, any second, to get lost, so he doesn't let go of his sons' hands. But he only has two hands, himself, so one of the children always needs to hold onto the end of his clothes. They take turns. They're already very good at it; they used to walk the same way through the streets of Netanya. But then, suddenly, one of the three vanishes. Just like that, disappears. In the blink of an eye. He can't tell me who the missing child is. I sit there and say to the other two children, this time it's serious—I recall that I've already dreamed this before, but nevertheless, I feel that it's not a dream this time. I remove my passport and see it's cut, and so I know that it's real. In the dream I don't know who's missing either, as if I can't see the faces of the two boys remaining with me. I go into a side room, there's a sort of engine room, I hear someone screaming from in there. A brown door, I remember. A narrow door. Like at the health clinic, in the x-ray department. And then a policeman comes up and asks, "Are you the owner?" I say to him, "Yes." And he looks at me with faint suspicion and asks, "Are you stopping here in Great Britain or do you also have business in . . . Sweden?" I don't understand him. The face of the policeman seems unforgiving, sealed off, and he says, "My good man, your son got on the plane to Stockholm. We hope you didn't arrange this." And then another policeman always arrives, tall, I think that he's ten feet tall in the dream, and on his shoulders sits the lost child. And someone says to me from somewhere by my side that I only need to raise my hands and take the boy down. But I just stand and look at him. I'm no longer afraid now—just angry. All of a sudden I'm terribly angry with the boy.

. . .

When a dog walks across the boulevard below, even when he's far away, Bob the guinea pig perceives the sound of its heavy breathing, which I only hear when the dog is very close. To me it sounds like wind blowing through small trees, but the guinea pig immediately retreats to his hiding place until the distant dog passes. In this way, this story is written.

. . .

I would sometimes meet him on a side path at the King's Garden. One can see the ancient port from the garden, in which there stands a Roman amphitheater, in which we once performed a children's version of *Oedipus the King*. There's a picture of me sitting on the steps, I'm the boy on the left, during rehearsals. On the stage a girl is pushing a stroller and in it is the limping child Oedipus, she is taking him to safety. The garden was an island of fog in the heart of Netanya. Thick trees, gravel trails, flowery walkways, silent grayish pools unclouded by anything save the movement of large goldfish scattered here and there. They say there's a river hidden on the grounds that runs from the King's Garden into the sea. How many hours we spent in our childhood searching for that river! And once we even found it. We didn't know then that the garden was named

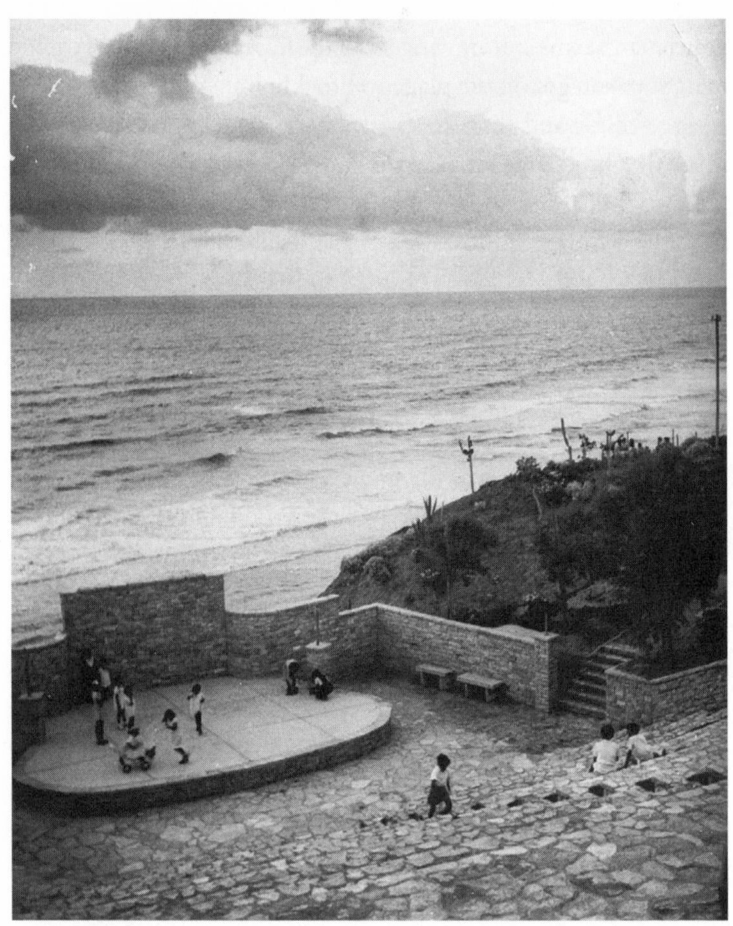

after the King of England, George the Fifth. We, the children, saw those two words—*the king*—as being without a clear referent. That's when I saw in the prayer book for the high holidays, the words *The King* with all its vowels written out and in thick black ink, I said to my father, "Like the King's Garden." And he smiled because he didn't know that I could read at all. And neither did I. But suddenly I identified the letters in the prayer book with the letters written in red flowers planted in the large bed at the entrance to the garden. And those were my first two words, even before I knew how to read and write my name.

When my grandfather retired, he would head down to the garden in order to "read the newspaper." Instead of going to work at the clinic, he would go to the King's Garden. He would examine each word closely, as if he were reading the Torah. I would follow my grandfather, at a distance of two to three meters. His hands behind his back, the palms of his hands, the hands of a carpenter, facing me: an uncertain form, like some sort of ancient creature newly emerged from the sea, moving his gills, breathing this strange, transparent, dry air. And sometimes he would stop, turn to me with a thought, or with a comment on something that was "in the newspaper," which was still rolled up and stuck under his armpit. For instance, "You understand . . . it took hundreds of years for us to be here walking and me telling you, 'You understand . . . it took hundreds of years for us to be here walking and me telling you . . .'" or, "Look, the wind from the sea . . . the wind comes from the sea like so and it touches, really touches, all the leaves of these trees. It's like saying 'the sea is touching the trees,' no?" And sometimes he would say more ambiguous things, like "There are many trees under these trees," or, "Rain on trees in the rain." And sometimes he would throw out a word, one single word whose meaning he no longer seemed to understand, a difficult word, like the word *iron*, and the word *orchard*, and the word *oven*, and the word *candlestick*, and the word *buckle*, and the word *divan*, and the word *shofar*, and the word *table*, and the word *hotel*, and the word *word*. "Buckle!" we would call out. Or combine two: "Buckle shofar!" "Orchard iron!" "Divan table!" Et cetera. These were his jokes.

In the heart of the garden, there would from time to time be archeological digs on behalf of the local antiquities authority. How ancient is our city. How fraught with secrets and eras. Bags of sand would be resting on the edge of their hole and a sheet of black fabric would be stretched over its mouth, to give the diggers some shade. In *This Week in Netanya*, it was written that the entire prehistory of the sea was located in this hole, sponges and nautiloids of all sorts, but also books and decorated pitchers and broken pomegranates that the inhabitants of Um Khalid didn't manage to take along when they fled for their lives. They're about to build a glass elevator in the garden that will slowly descend to the seashore. And on the way down you'll be able to see the past. Dolphins, mastodons, trilobites, copper pitchers, all the ancient inhabitants of Netanya. What an attraction. Years later I dreamed that I fell into this hole, and even though I knew I would certainly be crushed, and I already heard the sea drawing near, I opened my eyes to take in the fossils, but saw only more and more human skeletons. Layer upon layer of them, with only the colors of the earth changing.

Many years ago, our neighbor stood on the edge of the cliff and painted a view of the garden, picture after picture, doing the treetops with a brush dipped in green. But in time he would be sent to jail, and left to decorate the prison walls. And once, many years later, he exploited this and escaped, leaving behind a half-finished painting on a wall with barbed wire and sharp, colorful glass at its top. On the wall he'd painted a wall that birds were flying through. And from the road all of this looked entirely real. They caught him in the King's Garden, dressed up like a gardener, watering the flowers. After it was discovered that a resident of Netanya had been behind the kidnapping and murder, it was decided in the city council that the name of the garden would be changed to "Shimon Oded Garden" in honor of the victim. But the change proved too unpleasant a reminder, and the city inhabitants remained loyal to the original name. My grandfather dropped down onto a bench. The garden's ice cream man passed by on a distant path, and from his place stopped and watched us. "Vanilla?" he called out. "Vanilla!" my grandfather yelled back, and then turned to face me: "And you? What do you want?" But, in fact, I wasn't there at all, so ice cream was out of the question. Nevertheless, I said, "Get me exactly what you're getting for yourself." I asked him if he remembered the incident of the kidnapped boy. "Strange, you know?" he answered me. "When it was announced that they kidnapped him, I thought, certainly it's *you* who was kidnapped, not this other fellow. I was convinced of this. I knew in my heart that you were the one who'd been abducted. And this was well before they discovered who did it. I sat in our hotel, I think that this was in 1980, knowing that you'd been kidnapped and that they were demanding a ransom. I sat there on the moon balcony and didn't do a thing about it. I didn't call your parents, I didn't turn on the radio, I didn't yell out to the neighbors. I sat there silently and said to myself: The boy will be rescued. They won't kill him. Everything will be okay. Soon he will return home and eat ice cream with his parents. They'll laugh about everything that's happened. And I really heard the laughter."

. . .

"Look at this," my grandfather said in Yiddish to the florist, "one flower opens and already you can know that spring has arrived." The florist gave him the bouquet and said, "Dear Mr. Burstein. One leaf falls, and already you know that it's autumn." We placed the bouquet on my uncle's grave. A small box was there with a thick candle and long matches inside it. Each year, one match was burned. The candle was already an old candle, a twenty-year-old candle. We would light the old man and after a short time would blow him out. Inside this memorial candle box, resting on the box of matches, was a small stone, a basalt from Quneitra. My grandfather took it out once and showed it to us. We asked what it was exactly, and he said: "A black stone."

. . .

He would turn out the lights at home every night, "So that all the butterflies will leave."

. . .

With a match as big as a teaspoon my grandmother lit a fire and raised the light to me. This was in the hotel, but in the distant future or the distant past. And even if I wasn't awake when I saw it, I remember the light of the oil lamp and what was revealed to me by its light: a small candlestick on the windowsill, and in the candlestick always a braided *havdalah* candle, most of it consumed, and at its end two black, burned, slightly twisted wicks. Memorial candle. Certainly the light of the oil lamp was enough to reveal that there was nothing in the room other than a few dust-covered blankets, a pile of nailed boards, a smell of glue, and a giant clamp. And all Grandfather's saws were hanging on nails on the walls. Certainly there were around a hundred saws hanging there and about the same number of pliers. By the light of the candle. By the light of the candle and the match.

. . .

One day he went by himself to the military cemetery. But before he arrived at the grave,someone grabbed him, stuck a couple coins into his pocket and pulled him to another side of the graveyard, so that he could complete a *minyan*, a prayer quorum. An umbrella opened up over them. He didn't try to resist, was just dragged after the fellow, the coins rattling inside his jacket pocket. He also had a flashlight in his pocket, as always. And in a far corner, crowded under a tree, he saw the eight men waiting for them under eight identical umbrellas. "We are all his children," whispered the one dragging him. "I am the littlest. And he went and killed himself on us exactly today one year ago." My grandfather asked him, "Who are you?" And the man answered, "You know me."

. . .

Gunshots on Memorial Day. And speeches by the Minister of Defense (Deputy Minister of Defense). And "Remember" and "Blood of the Maccabees" stickers, which you always forget on your shirt, and which you find a few days later, already folded in the closet, after being laundered, and the sticker is still glued to it, torn, falling apart, faded. The flowers too have faded. And sometimes you don't see it in time and you go out onto the street like that. You're not the only one.

. . .

We dig for days, at a fixed time each day, sit crouched down on our digging stools, clutching tools, throwing the debris out of the hole. The layers of earth change their color, every few days our stools sink a bit more, the view keeps changing, new fossils pop up the further we descend into time, into the redness of time covered in earth. With soft white brushes we descend and clean dust off of bones and rocks. Every so often we lift our eyes to the distant edge of the hole, we've already gone half a meter down. How far the surface of the planet seems from here; we left our backpacks with our breakfasts up there! Oh, our hardboiled eggs—who knows if we'll ever see them again! We prick up our ears trying to hear talk from home, which grows more and more distant the more we dig away from it. Here below, the talk is different. We listen to the voice of the fossils that our brushes tickle after thousands of years of silence. The end of a tooth, an ancient fish scale. From time to time our brushes touch—we dig without stakes, without shovels—the faces of acquaintances, a creature like a forgotten aunt, or that same townsman who appeared in the hotel one day, presented a letter of recommendation, and without further ado stipulated the amount of money that would help him reach his destination—and if it's possible, just a day or two in the hotel, but these became months and years, until he changed the lock of an entire wing and declared it a separate kingdom, renting his rooms out to his own tenants, who—embarrassed—were brought inside via rope ladder, and even taking the name and reputation of the hotel for himself by announcing that he was the proprietor of "The *New* Hotel Tel Aviv," shouting "Vacancy! Vacancy! We have excellent rooms!" We look at all that, unearthed so close to the edge of the dig, the sign, the ancient guests stolen from my grandparents, the receipts that the man would carefully tear out of my grandfather's guestbook, tear out slowly, at night, in order not to make any noise. Behind every whitened thigh bone, behind every cracked tooth or shell stands a sort of distant relative, and he knows we're looking for him, and so when he sees us waving a brush in front of his face, and we shine the lights on our hardhats in his eyes, he rises, folds up his few possessions, and like a giant mole in a top hat and laced-up shoes digs further down and disappears deep into a layer of crumbling earth, as we follow slowly after. We want to chase after him, to grab him by the tail, to clutch him and ask him his name and what's new at home, but here we've already noticed another relative, a relative from another side of the family. He, too, is a sad story, he, too, dreamed a formidable dream, yes the earth is full of stories, and we are forced to pretend that we don't see him either.

. . .

In those days in Netanya, there were horse-drawn carriages. They parked next to Independence Square, and travelers to the port tended to show up in these carriages. There, in the square, horses ate from one big trough. Hay! Hay! the straw sellers called out, and the coachmen would descend from their seats, whips in hand, and go over to haggle. Since the large influx of immigrants from Russia in the seventies, Netanya's entire carriage sector is controlled by Russians, and thus the weight of straw is measured in poods, and its price in silver rubles (SR)—"Half a pood for seventeen silver rubles and fifty kopeks."—"Ho . . . add half a pood and be satisfied with ten SR and then I'll take out my wallet . . ." Beautiful piles of dung stood there in the square, and every coachman was required, according to a municipal bylaw ("Horse Dung and its Collection") to clean up whatever dung was directly in front of them (so everyone wanted to be first in line, in vain). One evening at the end of Yom Kippur, we returned from the Remez House synagogue, and a carriage stopped right next to us. The streets were empty. The coachman noticed a pile of dung and went over to clean it up. With a shovel he dug into the mound of feces and lifted it into the air. My grandfather approached the horse like a thief, looking this way and that, and from his suit pocket produced the large carrot that he'd brought along in order to break the fast. He always broke his fast with a carrot. He raised the carrot to the horse's teeth. It all happened so fast. My grandfather maintained a frozen expression, like a pickpocket. The horse also pretended that nothing was happening. The coachman suspected something, but what could he say? My grandfather withdrew his hand and hid it in the same pocket, and I too hid my hand in my pocket. The coachman also hid his hands in his pocket, as did the horse. From here on out, this thing became a custom for him. At the end of every Yom Kippur and Tisha B'av he would rush to feed the horses. How so many carrots, so many beautiful carrots, grew in his pocket was beyond my grasp. As if he had a carrot crop in there. He has a plot of farmland in his pocket, I thought. Pockets full of rich soil, which he aerates and waters. I was scared to check. I was scared to stick a hand into the soil in his pocket. There was always a horse, always a greeting, Russian to Polish, that is Yiddish, always opportunities to sneak over, always a large carrot, a mighty carrot, pulled from a grayish suit. And always there were hands eventually returning to pockets. Hungry, weak, worn out from prayer, my grandfather would take his first meal after the fast and deliver it to the beasts. On the windowsills of the hotel there was always dried bread in slices, pieces, crusts, and large crumbs, as though the hotel itself were an oven, and its windowsills—the bakery's shelves. And once, when we celebrated his ninetieth, he sliced half a cake, picked it up, and disappeared. He supported a few donkeys as well. But always and mainly horses. And precisely because the routine was repeated so many times, I'm starting to think that it never actually happened, like a dream recurring over and over again. In my memory, all the times become a single, unique time, and even that, now, fades and blurs so much, until nothing remains from all those performances but a single, limp, rotting, speckled, nearly black carrot, tossed deep inside the refrigerator inside my head.

. . .

Rosh Hashanah 2009. The hotel stands abandoned. The same tenant I mentioned earlier still resides there, but most of the wings have already been sealed up with gray cinderblocks. Doves nest on the roof that has folded up like paper. There is a large, formless mouth in Netanya, and it eats the floors and the rooms. Yesterday I asked my father if he has any old photographs of the hotel, from the thirties and forties, so that I could see how it was then, during its first years. He looked at me and said, "What do you need old photos for? Go and take pictures there today. I'll open the door for you. Not a thing has changed. Everything looks exactly like it did."

. . .

There was a room in our hotel with a large window that birds were allowed to fly into like a dovecote, and thus the season of migration above Netanya would commence and conclude in our hotel, and bird-watchers sat for hours at Café Whitman with binoculars and boxes of seeds, waiting for some rare songbird, and if you tossed half a loaf of bread in the air it wouldn't ever come back down; there was a room for officers of the Mandate and a special room for high-ranking representatives who would sometimes come for a night with the same actress always hanging on their arms, or the same famous singer, who for obvious reasons hid her face behind a Japanese Noh mask, one of those that would later be hung up in the theater room, and so in this way an "old man" or a "hungry spirit" or a "samurai" would pass the night next to a Brit in a brimmed hat and sandals; and then there was a memorial room for soldiers from the First World War decorated with pictures of soldiers from all the participating countries, along with poems that they'd written stuck inside the frames; and there was a room with maps and sketches that the "Old Man" labored over for days in an attempt to reimagine Netanya as an "ideal city," like those same imagined cities that a few Renaissance artists drew, cities of ruler and compass, empty of people except for the artist who drew them, cities open to wide vistas, full of air, and at their boundaries, sealed up by the ruler's thin line, the sea and the wind; another room contained a book whose pages were large and smooth and white, and numbered exactly one thousand (this was a failed edition of a King James Bible: The ink in the printing press ran out and all the pages remained blank), and the hotel guests would write in it, contributing to the hotel's long, serialized novel, and they would glue things onto its massive pages, like pictures, movie posters, and dried leaves, like revealing notes and convenience store receipts dripping with symbolic meanings, for example "½ loaf of bread—½ lira" or "low-fat cheese"; and then there was the not-very-large room, the small bedchamber where a laundry machine would eventually reside; and there was also a room with a talking flower, which my grandmother would water and exchange a few words with each time she passed by in the hallway ("*marhaba*"—"*marhabtayin* . . ."); and there was a small carpentry shop in a narrow room, in addition to the shed I've already mentioned a few times, but this room was impossible to use because it would disturb the guests' sleep, and they were always sleeping—and yet, once, the high commissioner, none other than Arthur Wauchope himself, who was an amateur carpenter, insisted on sinking a saw into a board and moving its teeth in that room, simply in order to get a hint, in his words, of that old, refined taste of "steel teeth in a fresh wooden board," and thus the hotel got an early wake-up call, and the board of sleep, as it were, was sawed clean through; and then there was a room containing a lettuce garden, beds of lettuce inside a room on the first floor, right under the bedchamber of that flower I've mentioned, and whoever entered the memorial room for the soldiers of the First World War would find himself, upon leaving, as when a dream changes subject or setting without warning or logic, among those beds of erect, Arab lettuce; and there was the Talmud room, where one could find a set of the Talmud that had come by itself, on foot, from Poland, brown books, heavy as weights, and every word, including the words of the commentators and the commentators on the commentators, gave off a strong scent, which nonetheless assaulted the newcomer like a persistent mumbling—as though the room itself was studying Talmud through the power of the presence of the books themselves; and then there was a room full of newspapers, and these were attached to these sorts of wooden poles, and there, a year before my birth, they read about man first landing on the moon; and there was a sea room, and in it a large pool that pipes kept filled with sea water, and sand had been brought up there too, warm as the sun and pleasant for wallowing in, and there were blue and yellow parasols stuck in the sand, and on summer days my father would work there as a lifeguard and once he saved me from drowning; and there was a water room, containing thirty or forty long, thin glasses, and thirty or forty faucets as well, connected to transparent glass tanks, and in each one of them there was always drinking water, imported from different places all around the world—water from Brazil and water from Germany, water from Poland and water from France, water from Japan and water from Uganda, and whoever had a little spare change on him could drink five or six glasses of cold water in one day, and my grandmother would stand next to him and declare: "Try from Turkey! Try from Afghanistan!" though all the countries would quench his thirst equally and he knew it, and while I was allowed to drink as much as I wanted from any of the tanks, I still preferred juice; and then there was a room dedicated to S. Y. Agnon, of whom my grandmother's father was patron and confidant in Germany, and I have in my possession the letters they wrote to one another in the twenties, and I will publish them someday with annotations and be promoted to the senior faculty; next to the water room was the room of clocks, which showed what time it was in all the distant water lands, and in order for their ticking not to annoy the guests in the other rooms, the clock room was draped in rugs—including the doors and the windows and the hands of the clocks; and then it's clear that some room, who knows where it was exactly—in my memory it hovers *above* the hotel completely—was allocated to worship, and in it was a Holy Ark and a Torah scroll in which one final *mem* had been copied incorrectly, but for some reason there was actually extra holiness in it, and therefore it was permitted in our hotel's synagogue despite the blemish, and therefore in our hotel's synagogue men and women were permitted to pray together, and non-Jews too, and fools too, and so it was; and there were rooms painted entirely in one color, white, for example, for no perceptible reason, just in order to celebrate as it were the existence of color—that is, to celebrate vision—that is, the universe in all its breadth, in all its depth; and of course there was the moon balcony; and then there was the candle room; there was a dark room and in it a table and some bottles, and this is where everyone would eat during bombing blackouts, which were declared once every few weeks in those days; and there was a room that was always empty and open; and there was a room with a paper screen in the middle . . . my grandfather carried a bundle of keys around with him, and each key had a name written on it, like "house" or "storeroom," "carpentry" or "shed," "St. Petersburg" or "belt factory;" and he had the key to our house too, never used, which had my father's name written on it; and he also had the key to my little Noah's ark-shaped bank, which he managed for me, and it was heavy with coins and even now serves as a doorstop for me so that the door won't close and anyone who wants to can come in; and then there was also a key strung onto the bundle that didn't have a thing written on it; and then there was also the broken key;

. . .

Today the moon started to revolve around the Earth in the opposite direction. It's inevitable, now, that the moon will crash into the Earth; it was supposed to happen within a hundred million years, perhaps less. But in the end it happened within two hours. We barely managed to pack up our things. In light, fluorescent running shoes, we flee, upright, running along fields of light, waving to the other refugees. They continue to run. A few of them, we are surprised to see, are flying, like geese, in flocks. The changes in gravity made them light. The light of the moon is already falling on their wings, on the streets. With rakes and steel shovels we clear it away, with large pumps we pump it and hurl it back at the sky.

. . .

There was a shaded pathway a bit behind the Bialik School, a short walk from our house. On today's map the pathway is called "Doctor Beckman," but for us it had no name, it was simply "the pathway." It connected Bialik Street, on which our house stood, and Dizengoff Street. We had a game: You took a deep breath before you stepped onto the pathway, and you held it in, as though you were about to dive underwater. And when we would emerge on the other end, out of breath and mouths wide to take some back in, we said to ourselves that we hadn't just walked through a bit of shade but rather through the Boulevard of Death; and it wasn't a half-minute of walking, it was a journey of a million years. And it was good to breathe again on the other side, in the atmosphere of Dizengoff Street. I was reminded of this pathway while I was on my bench, thinking about Peter Ward's book *Out of Thin Air*, which describes the history of planet Earth as a history of the changing quantity of oxygen in its atmosphere. Sometimes, he argues, there isn't enough oxygen and we gradually asphyxiate. Everything fades, silence prevails, a great death, millions of years of agony. My grandfather barked, "Every breath! Every breath!" and I too, on my bench, said, perhaps with my voice somewhat raised, perhaps even screaming, "Every breath!" He shouted these words and immediately covered his nose and mouth with an oxygen mask. Those were his last days. We have a heart inside of planet Earth, and its name is *core*; we have a lung around planet Earth, and its name is *atmosphere*. My heart was beating, and the dense, deep liquid below my feet moved a bit with the rhythm of my heartbeats. I inhaled air and exhaled, the blood and the air came and went without my making an effort, and in the heavens above, particles and bacteria moved too, took pains to make the air good for breathing. Doctors passed by in the corridor outside my grandfather's room and flapped their white wings. At a great height, writes Ward in his book, at the top of Everest, for instance, most human beings would die for lack of oxygen. But if they would only raise their heads before dying, they would see flocks of birds passing by far above them, far above the top of the mountain. "I can't bear to see a bird in a cage!" my grandfather said to me and again removed the mask from his mouth. "No-no! I can't! I can't! You must go and free them from all those horrible stores! Promise me you'll go store to store! Break the glass if you have to! And dive in and crack the deep-sea fish cages open too!" He put the mask back on and breathed for a few minutes, and because I thought that he'd fallen asleep, I got up to go, but he removed the mask once more and looked at me and said, "I chose your name—I said, it has to be the name of a bird. Before you go, if it isn't too much trouble, give me two drops in the left eye?" From my place on the bench I looked at my car, I touched the key in my pocket and said to myself, you have to get up, in a moment the garbage truck will pass by, in a moment all the street cleaners will fill up the boulevard. I heard the panting of a dog at the end of the street and I knew that, above, my guinea pig was hurrying to hide. I too panted. I looked at the trees on the boulevard and they looked at me. I exhaled—they inhaled. Slowly they grew, and their roots reached places where there is no oxygen but where there are very small animals, which are always laboring over something important that no one knows about and no one can see. Yet thanks to them we live. This too is a part of breathing. I breathed, I didn't think anything. When they chopped down the tree in front of the Hotel Tel Aviv, before finally demolishing the hotel, a demolition that was delayed for administrative reasons which are still unclear today—the bulldozer was parked in the parking lot for a decade, waiting for instructions—my grandfather said that they'd really cut down only a fraction of the thing, that its real branches were stuck underground, where it wasn't possible to chop them down. It passes from the air to the ground, and not the other way around, he said. It doesn't feel the chainsaw at all. This I tell you as a carpenter, he said. Think about all those roots, the dark fruits are there. Think about all the apples in the dark, deep down, that no one eats. I once ate apples from there, he said and fell silent. I picked up Peter Ward's book *Out of Thin Air* from the chair next to his sickbed. I wanted to show him the graph on page thirty, the cruel drop in oxygen at the end of the Permian as well as at the end of other periods, following which mass extinctions always took place. In the graph, at the end of each drop in oxygen, is a cross signifying an extinction. But my grandfather had already closed his eyes and fallen asleep, and regardless didn't believe in those epochs. He knew—and it was a fact—that the world had been created only five or six thousand years ago. On the bench, I recalled Ward's graph, how after each cross the oxygen rises, and there is breathing again. We breathe and change together and are born again as different creatures. Suddenly we are covered in fur, suddenly we sprout wings, suddenly we're in the depths of the sea, luckily we don't recognize ourselves. How much we've changed. Some device beeped. On the bench I recalled how, from the other end of corridor, three doctors hurried by. A small bird that was trapped in the ward cleared the way to the beds.

. . .

After I got that sewing-machine needle stuck in my finger, I needed to get a shot. And so I arrived one morning at the "Um

Khalid" branch of the National Health Service, where my grandfather was a clerk. "Come early, come at six, it's always worth it to be first in line," he said. But at six there were already twenty sick people there, and most of them had already been there since four, and actually they'd wanted to come at three, but they restrained themselves. A man in need of a nurse or a doctor, my grandfather said, will do everything in order to reach the seat that's next to their office door. The bench next to the door is already half a doctor, and in many instances—an entire doctor. We sit on the bench next to the doctor's door and already think, maybe it was a mistake to come—why, we already feel much better! Truth be told, we become healthy as a bull at the mere sight of a doctor's closed door and nameplate. Here at the clinic, many things become clear. At five in the morning, three hours before the medical staff arrives, patients are already standing outside, next to the gate, stomping their feet from the cold. They point at the stars and are already dreaming about the pharmacy and the pharmacist who will glance at the prescription they've yet to receive and go over to the cabinet to fetch the medicine. There is medicine in a drawer already waiting for everyone, and they need only narrow the gap between themselves and it. Narrow, close, and swallow. They are far from the medicine, but they move slowly in its direction, and soon they will receive it. The end is good, always. Always. In the end, silence always comes and it's possible to close the book and return it to the shelf. So the one who comes first brings along a piece of paper and a pen with a small spring—the first in line always have a piece of paper and a pen with a spring!—to make a list. At the top of the page he writes the date and then as many numbers as will fit, in a vertical line, putting his own name next to the number 1. A man writes his name on a doctor's waitlist with such care. So beautiful are the letters, so clear. There is no joy like the joy of the list maker, who is also the first in line. No one will get by him, there's no chance. The list is his. The pen is his.

And the paper. He makes the laws today. When the next in line comes, the first will ask him his name and will *himself* add his (the second's) name to the list. At the clinic, people speak gently to one another, and their courtesy lasts so long as the list is obeyed. And it is obeyed—I'm responsible for that. At the clinic at five in the morning the people arrive at themselves, at the silence they looked forward to at length. In the weak light of damp lamps one can see them for what they are: small mice of rain. Butterflies of shoes. Flies of sweet fruit. Weak as dew. How much tension is released the moment their names are added to the list, said my grandfather, and I repeated his words, not exactly, as I lay on the bench that was gradually filling up with light, light that was no longer in the sun, at a distance of one hundred and fifty million kilometers from Earth, but absorbed now, inside our mumbling mouths, touching our eyes and calling to them, saying *open for me*. And the eyes pass quickly over the names on the list, to see if any are familiar, as one does with the obituary column in the paper in line at the dentist. But here the names live, they live! And we know that around eight, someone will come, he always comes, who only wants a "little prescription," or has a "small question," and then there's the one who "just wants to show the x-ray to the doctor, look, I'll stop right here in the doorway, I won't even come in, look" (but slowly, slowly "steals in," see, a leg has already slipped inside, and now the door's slammed shut), or the one who "had a fever this morning," who just doesn't "feel well," who's having "complications" (and the response to this, the wording absolutely uniform: "As if *we* feel good! Who here doesn't have a hundred and one, a hundred and two?"), or who says "I was already here." (And the response: "Of course: clearly. All of us, *all of us* were already here. Sit, sit.") And they understand, they don't get mad at the newcomer—they just point quietly at the list, hearts filled with compassion: how predictable, how pitiful the effort, doomed in advance. They give him the pen, the sound of the released spring is heard in the corridor, and they point at the list. And he lowers his head, accepts defeat, and sits down. They know me, my grandfather said, who sat at the menorah's height, next to the chimneys. Even though I'm only a reception clerk, they tell me what brought them and what hurts and show me all their documentation. And I give them advice, and sometimes they're satisfied with this and go home to sleep, and even before the sun is up they are already settled back in bed, recovering. Twenty years, day after day behind that wooden counter, you learn a lot about healing and sick people, I said to myself, repeating what he told me then. He sat there behind the counter, and next to him, to his right, was a large box full of *cottin* balls. My grandfather said *cottin* balls and not cotton balls, and my father says *cottin* balls and I say *cottin* balls and so will all the readers of this book, now and forever. And the old people would approach me, he said, to ask who was seeing patients that morning, but the question was just a pretext. Actually they came to me in order to receive medical advice, and even first aid, since most of their illnesses did not exist, they went to the clinic like to a country club, like you'd go today to the mall out of boredom. Their only real illness was boredom, the inability to sit at home alone for half an hour, with themselves and only themselves. No, they rushed out to the hospital first thing in the morning. And my grandfather would wait for them there with the giant box of *cottin* balls, which a child could've climbed inside to sleep, as indeed once happened. The patients would lean on my grandfather's counter and ask for advice, taking out and lining up their aches on the counter one by one like polished diamonds on a velvet tray and my grandfather would diagnose them and even treat them on the spot with *cottin* balls. He would give them larger or smaller doses of *cottin* balls according to the severity of the ache, allot them a dose of *cottin* balls according to his own deliberations: for this one a bit of *cottin* ball to insert in an infected ear; for that one a handful of *cottin* balls to wet in the weak, warm tea that he blanched himself in the samovar at the end of the corridor to place on that eye dribbling with the morning's fresh pus; for this one a cubit of *cottin* balls to absorb menstrual blood; and for that one whole cords of *cottin* balls to rub with apple vinegar from the kitchen and place between the toes infected with seething eczema. The old people would approach him an hour or two before the doctors came, and he would allot them some *cottin* balls, and ninety percent of the time, he said to me proudly, by the time the doctors showed, no additional treatment was necessary. Ninety percent of diseases can be healed with the help of *cottin* balls and a little attention, he said, and absentmindedly pulled a few *cottin* balls from the box and gave them to me. "Take," he said. "You'll need it after she pricks you."

Here you understand everything about people, he said. Here all the masks fall away. Why, it's like Carnival in Brazil. The poor, the rich, the learned, the insane, the successful, the failures, the clerks, the carpenters—everyone dances a samba together, he said, and moved his hands like a dancer. Chaka-chak, he said, chaka-chuk. Chaka-chak, chaka-chuk, so he said—verbatim. Here too we have our dance. Don't laugh, yes, there's a clinic dance. Only it's slower, sadder. They come. And they write down their names. And they sit as close as they possibly can and look at the door and the list. And every few minutes they get up to check if their names are still on the list. And they come up to me in order to get *cottin* balls. And they read their documentation for the hundredth time: the referral and the x-ray and blood count and prescriptions. What intense concentration, what piercing memorization. They read only this. No books, no newspapers, not even Health Service pamphlets. This is what people want to read, their medical documents. And, look, if they actually do themselves a favor and open a book, they still want the book to have some connection to their medical file, to promise them recovery, good health. Even the severely sick, even the *incarables*. That's all. And yes, you're supposed to say inc*u*rables, my grandfather said, but I say *incarables*, and my mistake is not a mistake, yes I myself am *incarable*. And then the moment always arrives in which another dancer goes to the dance floor to dance with both the *incarables* and the regular sick people. And like the way you would peek at someone's book, at the beach, to try and flirt with them a little bit, the other dancer has a look and says, "That x-ray, well well . . . it doesn't look so good to me, ay-ay-ay." And then one sick person becomes the doctor of the sick person next to him, and he asks, "Did you get *cottin* balls already?" And points at me. And, as with a plague, it's contagious, they give one another medical advice and compare medications and blood pressures and histories. And if they have any leftover *cottin* balls they give them to their fellow man. It's like in Brazil, they forget who they were, it's first names only, Yankele or Avrum, they become anonymous, blend completely together, because they know that beyond those names they're all the same, are just "the human species," which at one time has a name like this and another time has a name like that, and their illnesses are all the same illness as well, maybe once your head hurt on the right side and once on the left side, but it's always a "headache," and anyway all illnesses are actually mental illnesses. My diabetes and my smoking are both mental illnesses, my grandfather said, I acquired them on the day that Shalomke was killed, he said and then went quiet for a time. You certainly don't remember him, he added. So I love my diabetes and love my smoking. You understand: They're mementoes. Each cigarette, each shot. Golda made a miscalculation, Dayan winked his good eye, and here I am, among the sick. I'm barely alive. I want to scream every day but I do not scream. I scream but I do not scream. Sometimes when I scream I do not scream and sometimes when I do not scream I scream. I say these things to you now and now too I want to scream but I do not scream. I scream. I do not scream. He said, I scream, I do not scream, and on the bench I mumbled "I scream," and "I do not scream," and for a moment I thought about getting up and kicking the bench in, cracking its wood like bones, but I didn't scream and I didn't get up even though after so many years here it's impossible not to scream. And I remembered that monkey from my childhood notebook, the one floating in black space holding a green apple in his hand, and below him are planet Earth and all its forests, and I covered my face with the palms of my hands. The clinic. Sitting on broken benches. And everyone wants to give help and everyone wants help. Here this is clear. They love it because they know that at the clinic they're allowed to be themselves, their true selves. Like at Carnival in Rio, they move their buttocks, they move their thighs, they don't care too much what others will say: They're sick. They're allowed to dance. At home they'll no longer dance. Here they will. I see them every day, I know each one, first name, last name, and their entire medical file, including regular medications and allergies. I say to you that they come here not for the doctor or the nurse but rather for the other sick. They are sick people and they love the other sick people like a dancer loves another dancer. They can dance the samba together here, with all the bandages and eardrops and *cottin* balls that they immediately shove into their ears and noses. Everyone gets a mustache here, look. They love to put the balls in their noses and ears, I can't explain it. But I understood, after ten years at Um Khalid, that there's nothing more important than illness. Illness gives us an opportunity to recall who we truly are. Only one who was sick and became healthy can be considered healthy. I saw a man who came to get his thumb bandaged after it was cut while he was slicing eggplants. It had become white with bandages, and at the same moment a deep change occurred in the man that he only managed to understand a few years later. He said to me, a week after the bandaging of my thumb I saw my handwriting and it had changed beyond recognition. The bandaging changed my handwriting because I was forced to hold the pen differently and also write more slowly. And then I saw that my new handwriting resembles, no, not "resembles," *is identical to*, my mother's handwriting. For years I tried to hide this without knowing it, but the bandages removed the camouflage and my true handwriting was revealed. I sat down at the table and wrote my mother a letter, for the first time in my life, and I remembered my grandfather telling me about this same patient, and I rubbed my back against the bench a bit. From far away I heard the cleaners' carts ascending Louis Marshall Street, which runs perpendicular to the boulevard. I knew that I had only a few more seconds, that in a bit I'd have to get up from the bench, grab my book-cum-headrest, and disappear. And now that I knew that my time was limited, I held onto the bench like a drowning man. Here at the clinic, my grandfather said, taking a look at his watch, important changes happen each and every day. Or they don't happen. Mostly they don't happen. But sometimes a man comes, and a seriously ill person for some reason gives up his place in line for him, and the seriously ill person gets better. The truly-healthy remembers his illness in days of health like a man would remember once being blind, and I once saw a man here like that, he remembered the blackness that was all he saw for many years each time he closed his eyes. With every blink he had a terrible reminder. Every time his eyes closed, and every time they opened. One needs a reminder like that—today I understand. This morning, he said suddenly, I saw that winter arrived. I opened my shoe drawer and from out of a shoe came a black butterfly. Or a moth. I got a reminder, he said, and pointed at the pack of cigarettes and the vial of insulin resting next to one another by a fountain pen on his table. A dog entered, followed by someone with a deep gash on his cheek. The man stood in front of us and asked, "Who's last in line for the nurse?" My grandfather looked at him for a long time, as if he knew him and was trying to recall from where, but couldn't, until he gave up and just answered: "This boy here," and then pointed at the list stuck to the door. I turned my head, and then I saw, near the yellow placard, written in my grandfather's handwriting: *1. Dror Burstyn*, up at the top of the white sheet of paper.

. . .

Silent green leaves at six in the morning. All this summer, every morning, I thought about Netanya. I don't know why. Years later, the city suddenly returns, the city suddenly calls out to you. And you're already on your way. And you're already in the city. Your hands swell from vaccine, your thumb is bandaged and disrupts your writing, beautifies your script. Silent leaves in the light. The smell of Netanya's sea, which no one bathes in yet, rests on the blinds. The sand is raked smooth by the morning wind's rakes. But if you move closer you can see the imprint of an ear on the surface of the sand. And the footprints of birds, barely visible, that were left behind, a flock of sea sparrows. A line of footprints, four-toed, continues until they reach the ear dug in the sand, dug into the earth, but dug into the sky spread close above it as well. And into it we will flap and finally take off.

. . .

I rose from my bench. The time was already six thirty or seven, but there was no one on the boulevard. Not the street cleaners, who'd passed me by without so much as a glance, not my neighbors, not the few remaining worshipers who turned up at the large, gradually abandoned synagogue. No one was outside. On the bench facing mine, someone had abandoned a pile of entirely new clothing. On the other side was the wall of a residential building facing west, and it was still dark as night. I rose from the bench too quickly and almost fainted from dizziness. *Rare Earth* slipped from my hand and fell. A man lies down for hours and then suddenly stands. I recalled a trick that my grandfather taught me, unless it was my neighbor who got a life sentence and is still in jail: When you have a bad dizzy spell, you must look at a single point, a star or a flower for example, whatever happens to be in sight, until it passes. And it has to pass eventually. So I turned around and looked at the sign on my house, at the number 18. I focused my gaze upon the top of the black 8. Then I went over to my car, opened the door, and climbed in. The door slammed into me on its own. I held the steering wheel tightly. I wanted to rest my forehead on the steering wheel. So much cold here, that the car collected overnight. Two hundred thousand kilometers in a bit, the odometer declared. There was a beautiful morning light. From somewhere to my right, I heard a shutter smack into a drainpipe. I remembered my grandfather had a large tin pail with the word *rain* written on it in black letters. I saw that I was still holding the steering wheel of my car. All of a sudden—reality.

July–September 2009

Books Mentioned in *Netanya*

Jared Diamond, *Guns, Germs, and Steel: The Fates of Human Societies*, W. W. Norton & Company, 2005.

Sebastian Haffner, *Defying Hitler: A Memoir*, Oliver Pretzel trans., Picador, 2003.

Thich Nhat Hanh, *The Song of No Coming No Going*, LNEB, 1996.

—, *Touching Peace*, Parallax, 2009.

Ian Kershaw, *Hitler*, 2 Vols. W. W. Norton & Company, 2000, 2010.

Yoram Kupermintz, *October: War Diary*, Babel, 2000.

Maurice Maeterlinck, *The Life of the Bee*, University Press of the Pacific, 2001 [1901].

Chet Raymo, *The Soul of the Night*, Cowley Publications, 2005.

Henrik Svensmark & Nigel Calder, *The Chilling Stars: A New Theory of Climate Change*, Totem Books, 2003.

Peter D. Ward & Donald Brownlee, *Rare Earth: Why Complex Life Is Uncommon in the Universe*, Springer, 2003.

—, *The Life and Death of Planet Earth*, Times Books, 2003.

Peter D. Ward, *The Call of Distant Mammoths*, Springer, 1998.

Peter D. Ward, *Gorgon*, Viking, 2004.

—, *Life as We Do Not Know It*, Viking, 2005.

—, *Out of Thin Air*, Joseph Henry Press, 2006.

—, *Under a Green Sky*, Collins, 2008.

Avot Yeshurun, *Homograph*, Hakibbutz Hameuchad,1985.

Translator's Afterword

Perhaps the most surprising moment in David Grossman's ambitious and widely read 2008 novel, *To The End of the Land*, comes at the very end, in its final line. Here it is, along with the rest of the paragraph that precedes it:

> Then Ora detaches her body from his and lies down on her side on the rock ledge. She pulls her knees into her stomach and rests her cheek on her open palm. Her eyes are open yet she sees nothing. Avram sits beside her, his fingers hovering over her body, barely touching. A light breeze fills the air with the scents of *za'atar* and poterium and a sweet whiff of honeysuckle. Beneath her body are the cool stone and the whole mountain, enormous and solid and infinite. She thinks: how thin is the crust of Earth.[1]

I find this novel's final moment perfectly arresting, since here—after 576 richly detailed pages, pages that present the reader with a nearly exhaustive portrait of its main characters in their social and historical context—Grossman offers us a radically new vantage point from which to consider his fictional world. With this final gesture, the narrator does nothing more and nothing less than present Ora in her *geological* context. By emphasizing, of all things, the *thinness* of the Earth's crust, Grossman rotates the narrative's orientation ninety degrees. In other words, the novel's final note draws our attention to the Earth's vertical axis, though it does this precisely by mentioning its upper most layer, the crust. This is the horizontal axis along which Ora desperately escapes and across which her husband Ilan bravely

1. David Grossman, *To The End of The Land*, trans. Jessica Cohen (New York: Knopf, 2010), 576.

marches during the 1973 Yom Kippur War and in which her lover Avram (and the rest of the characters—including, possibly, the dead ones) remain tragically stuck.

Covering forty years, Grossman's *To The End of the Land* is exactly the kind of wide-canvas historical novel that modern Hebrew literature (like virtually all modern national literatures) has aspired to for over a century, but has rarely realized. Grossman meticulously situates the lives of his characters within Israeli history since 1967, masterfully blending the macro (the political, the historical, and the social) with the micro (the familial, the personal, and the psychological) in the process. And, of course, such comprehensive blending of these two extremes is something that virtually all great novelists—Dickens, Tolstoy, Joyce, Faulkner—have in common.

For this reason—and despite all its interest in *erets* in its many, many senses[2]—Grossman's novel has done little to prepare his reader for this final moment. Ora is suddenly dwarfed by the vastness of planet Earth, and with our perspective radically altered the entire human drama—including the Israeli one—is rendered rather trivial in the scheme of things. Here Grossman both escalates the novel's escapist thrust[3] (to hell with the surface of the Earth, along with all the people on it) and compels us to view his whole massive narrative as somehow miniscule as well. In other words, this conclusion is arguably a subtle admission of a fundamental absurdity informing the supposedly epic terms of this novel as a whole, an especially remarkable move in a work that would seem to embody the greatest aspirations of national literature.

2. *Erets* can be translated as "country," "land," "territory," "ground," "soil," "earth," and "world." When used with the definite article, "The Land" (*ha-arets*), it functions as a synonym for Israel. I doubt it's coincidence that *erets* is in fact the last word of Grossman's novel.

3. Though it includes numerous extended flashbacks, the present of Grossman's novel narrates Ora fleeing from her home in order to be absent if and when representatives of the army arrive to inform her of her son's death.

But what if, as Grossman intimates here, the two poles of Israeli life (the historical and personal) don't actually represent the true edges of anything? In particular, what if the macro of modern Israeli history (and modern Middle Eastern geography) isn't so macro after all? What would happen if a writer stretched the macro all the way out to the spatial and temporal limits of the universe in its entirety? Could such a macro be blended with literature's standard micro? And what would happen if this writer didn't wait until the final line of his book to destabilize the conventional dimensions of national culture, but instead opened with this gesture and then sustained it for two hundred pages? Dror Burstein's *Netanya* is an effort to confront questions like these, and the results are unlike anything I have ever read.

Netanya, which probably contains too much explicit autobiography to be called a novel,[4] opens with an epiphany: Burstein has been reading, "with an amazement that turned, on occasion, into awe," *Rare Earth*, by the American scientists Peter D. Ward and Donald Brownlee. Briefly, *Rare Earth* argues that though simple life may be quite common throughout the universe, an improbably vast set of astrophysical and geological events and conditions is necessary for the type of complex life that exists here on Earth. Laying down on a street bench near his home in Tel Aviv, Burstein states his epiphany:

> How flimsy our existence is, how many conditions *must exist and must continue to exist over the course of millions of years* so that a single flower or a single pencil or a single book might exist. . . . For a moment I felt like a string being strummed by thousands of fingers, and I closed my

4. Netanya was not classified as either memoir or fiction when published in Israel. In an e-mail, Burstein writes that "I guess 'prose' is the most agreeable term."

> eyes. Our existence on this planet hangs by a thread, every tomato and every onion is such an enormous miracle you could collapse with awe in a vegetable market.

Netanya is Burstein's effort to recreate the night he spent on this bench, which, not surprisingly, includes extensive reflections on the "rare Earth" hypothesis and a host of related scientific works. Indeed, like much of Hebrew literature, *Netanya* is positioned within a thick intertextual web, but here Burstein conducts a dialogue not with Hebrew novels such as Brenner's *Breakdown and Bereavement*, Shamir's *He Walked Through the Fields*, or Shabtai's *Past Continuous*, but rather with scientific studies such as *Life as We Do Not Know It*, *The Chilling Stars*, and *The Call Of Distant Mammoths*.

And yet *Netanya* is much more than an Israeli writer's reflection on this collection of decidedly thought-provoking research. All this represents only *Netanya*'s macro extreme, but there is a micro as well. Burstein introduces his version of the micro by recalling, early on, that he studied astronomy and built a telescope at the age of fourteen. *Netanya* thus opens up into a memoir, one that will alternate with, reflect on, and be read against Burstein's commentaries on the above-mentioned science. One of the great pleasures of reading Burstein's book is following the author as he cleverly and regularly shuttles between these two vastly distinct extremes,[5] between the cosmic and the human.

---

5. For the sake of accuracy, it should be noted that Burstein's micro in fact reaches the literally microscopic in places, where he discusses microbes, bacteria, etc. Indeed, the "text" *Netanya* most resembles may be the short 1977 documentary film, *Powers of Ten*, which presents the universe according to a logarithmic scale based on a factor of ten. Beginning with a one-meter square overhead image of a couple picnicking in Chicago, the film steadily zooms out until the square reaches 10^{24} meters, or 100 million light years across. The film then gradually zooms in until reaching 10^{-16}, or the space inside a single proton. The kind of pleasant, if humbling, disorientation I experienced after watching that film as a child in some science museum somewhere came back to me more than once while reading Burstein's book. The entire film is now available on YouTube.

Burstein employs a number of strategies to facilitate this shuttling, some more obvious than others. In addition to the episodes in his biography that find him as an amateur astronomer, there are moments of coincidence, such as the fact that his grandfather reached an Immigrant Center in Palestine on the same date (but not the same year) that rays from an exploded magnetar (a giant star) reached Earth: August 27th. But the dialogue between the human and the cosmic grows most interesting in *Netanya* when their relationship becomes metaphorical. For instance, Burstein writes about a third of the way through the book:

> All of these, my uncle's death, the boy's murder, my grandfather's watches, they are planets in my solar system or in what I could call my universe, which is in fact every person's universe, just as the universe of each person is my universe as well, just as the sun is part of the solar system but by the very same measure is part of a galaxy and a cluster of galaxies and the universe. I was not at the center of these things, but they had exerted their pulls on me just as I certainly had exerted mine on them.

This metaphorical language resonates strongly with the reader for a couple of reasons. First, after already spending over fifty pages steeping in the profundity of the planets, the stars, and the whole universe, the reader has been primed by Burstein himself to decode this kind of figurative language as particularly, perhaps uniquely, meaningful. Second, and more important, the reader can't help but suspect, and ultimately conclude, that much of the figurative language isn't in fact figurative at all.

What Burstein is advancing here—and this is one of the book's central themes—is not just, as the cliché goes, that everything is connected, but that every thing is absolutely part of every other thing. The first appearance of "universe" in this passage functions within an extended metaphor, but by its fourth mention "universe" has become the actual, literal universe, which Burstein suggests he is an integral part of.[6] In other words, Burstein, while reconstructing his childhood and his night on the bench, consistently strives to position them within the largest conceivable contexts: the history of the Earth and the universe as a whole. For this reason, when Burstein writes, "I closed my eyes, raised my hands, and felt Jupiter's gravity pull at my fingernails and lengthen them," he's not merely being playful, that is, if he's being playful at all.

And while Burstein makes these kind of far-reaching, nearly counterintuitive claims again and again, there is also something matter-of-fact about his presentation. As he writes elsewhere, "This book is written by a living man with the help of many dead, and this proclamation is perfectly obvious, I think, and not the least bit mystical." Though it may not be mystical, this book has an unmistakably spiritual undercurrent. Burstein grew up in a religious Jewish home, and though he would now be described—in Israeli terms—as secular, there's no question that the kind of transcendent thinking associated with religion remains evident throughout *Netanya*. Only now it appears to be of a decidedly eastern variety. Burstein quotes the Vietnamese Zen teacher Thich Nhat Hanh for three straight pages here, presenting Hanh's claim that on the largest scales there is no such thing as birth and death, but only manifestations of continuity.

This combination of the profound and the direct is Burstein's expression of another Zen term, *tathata*, sometimes translated as "suchness." As Alan Watts writes:

> The Sanskrit word *tat* (our "that") is probably based on a child's first efforts at speech, when it points at something

6. Elsewhere he writes, "The ends of my net are connected to the nets of every human being and of every thing. There is only one net."

> and says, "Ta" or "Da." . . . *Tathata* therefore indicates the world just as it is, unscreened and undivided by the symbols and definitions of thought. It points to the concrete and the actual as distinct from the abstract and conceptual. A Buddha is a Tathagata, a "thus-goes," because he is awakened to the primary, nonconceptual world . . .[7]

Netanya opens with Burstein's suddenly unmediated recognition of the unlikely and unmistakable reality of all life, and by extension, existence. The suchness of truly everything. Though this might seem to be an abstraction, it isn't at all, since for the duration of the book Burstein remains facing the night sky and the universe beyond it as things absolutely present and concrete. He is, in a sense, *pointing* at all of this. As Watts notes, "When we say just 'That' or 'Thus,' we are pointing to the realm of the nonverbal experience, to reality as we perceive it directly, for we are trying to indicate what we see or feel rather than what we think or say."[8] In other words, Burstein's epiphany can be understood as the experience of simply feeling this invisible, boundless abstraction transform into a physical, palpable actuality. I read *Netanya* in large part as his ambitious effort to articulate this universal, transcendent suchness in such a way as to render it perfectly ordinary (in part by integrating it with the conventionally quotidian)—to, in other words, demystify what is so often confused with mysticism.

And yet it is precisely the combination of this all-embracing, cosmic suchness with the details of Burstein's biography and family history that give the latter their force. In regards to the macro, *Netanya* is front-loaded. The reader encounters fewer and fewer references to science as the book progresses; but these later, comparatively more familiar pages are no less powerful than what

7. Alan Watts, *The Way of Zen* (New York: Vintage, 1999), 67–68.
8. Ibid, 67.

comes first. Some of this effect, of course, has to do with the atypically vast context in which his personal and familial past have been situated. But much of the force of these sections has to do with Burstein's skill as a writer in more traditional senses. Burstein's approach to memory, his project of reconstructing his family's participation in the drama of Zionism and Israel, are both terribly poignant. In this regard, his contribution to the trend of the memoir in Hebrew literature[9] should be read as an intervention as well.[10]

The best-known Hebrew memoir by far is Amos Oz's 2002 *A Tale of Love and Darkness*, widely considered one of modern Hebrew literature's greatest achievements. This work's status may be explained in part by the fact that Oz's sweeping memoir reasserts a decidedly epic Zionist and Israeli narrative. Oz is able to construct this kind of story by virtue of the way his biography intersects with national history. Born in 1939, Oz witnessed the declaration of Israeli independence, lived on a kibbutz, and achieved literary renown in the second half of the 1960s. In other words, his personal story overlaps with the realization of Zionism and the growth—and later expansion—of the state itself. However critical in places, Oz presents his readers with an Israel they have come to expect (and quite possibly now long for).

Burstein, by contrast, was born two literary generations later. Though the reconstruction of his family history includes numerous recognizable and even quintessential moments from the Zionist and Israeli story (immigration to Palestine, fighting in its wars, etc.), the overall effect is radically different than that produced by

9. In addition to Oz's work (discussed below), see Haim Be'er's *The Pure Element of Time* along with Yoram Kaniuk's *1948* and *Life on Sandpaper*.

10. Burstein, who has a PhD in Hebrew Literature and teaches at Tel Aviv University, explicitly views this book as an intervention in Hebrew literature as a whole. In at least a half-dozen places in these pages he mentions—tongue perhaps in cheek at times—how little Hebrew literature has had to say about the "big picture" (i.e., absolutely everything).

A Tale of Love and Darkness. Burstein's work is fragmented and achronological, there is barely a narrative here at all, but rather, as Burstein himself calls them, a series of "sketches." But more than this is the fact that Burstein's childhood, instead of being surrounded by birth and growth, is informed by decay, death, and a single instance of decades-long mourning.

The central space of Burstein's childhood is the family-run hotel, which devolves into a ruin before his very eyes. The family's dominant encounter with key dates in the national narrative comes in the form of his uncle's death in 1973. In what might be called a thoroughly post-Zionist gesture, Burstein never once weighs in on the political implications of this death or this war, at least not in recognizable terms. The closest he comes to commentary—once again expanding the scope of his prose—is to view war as a manifestation of the human "extinction impulse." In lieu of politics, Burstein recounts, again and again, the way this death left a lasting mark on his grandfather, Zvi Burstein, who entered his "ice age in October 1973."

Indeed, Burstein's grandfather is—along with Burstein himself—this book's true protagonist, and one of the more memorable characters (fictional or not) I've come across in Hebrew literature in some time. A central presence throughout Burstein's childhood—he appears here much more than either of Dror's own parents—this grandfather infuses the memoir with a tender, haunting melancholy. The younger Burstein is raised in (and perhaps raised *by*) the loving shadow of his grandfather's steady mourning and slow decline, though the tragedy of the former and the sorrow in the latter are rarely if ever named directly. In other words, Burstein never exploits his grandfather's situation in order to manipulate the reader emotionally. His grandfather was simply a looming feature of his childhood landscape, a diminished but still lofty suchness in the larger suchness of Burstein's fragmented past.

The great interpretive challenge of *Netanya* is deciding quite how to reconcile Burstein's extreme oscillation between the cosmic and the human. How are we to view this more familiar family history against the boundless backdrop erected by the book's astronomical opening? What is the meaning of Burstein's childhood and family history in the face of the Rare Earth hypothesis, and, for that matter, vice versa? One of the great pleasures of *Netanya* is sitting with this arguably unanswerable question, of simply being compelled to try and produce a response. What is certain is that the contrast between the two extremes is only heightened by the fact that Burstein presents the cosmic with grateful wonder, whereas he reconstructs his biography with sober melancholy. Burstein's extended experiment here makes the reading of *Netanya* an encounter with a very existential defamiliarization, of suddenly seeing everything—yes, everything—in a wholly new light. The success of this defamiliarization can be measured by the way Burstein destabilizes the meaning of the book's final word. The novel concludes with Burstein standing up from the bench as morning begins. After a brief spell of dizziness, he walks to his car, unlocks it, and sits down inside. Here are the last two sentences: "I saw that I was holding my car's steering wheel. All of sudden—reality." It's hard to know exactly what Burstein intends to suggest with this last word, but what is clear is the word can't possibly mean for the reader quite what it meant before opening *Netanya*.

Todd Hasak-Lowy
2013

Dror Burstein was born in 1970 in Netanya, Israel, and lives in Tel Aviv. He teaches literature at Tel Aviv University, used to edit classical music programs for Israel Radio's music station, and writes literary and art reviews. He has been awarded the Bernstein Prize (2005) and the Prime Minister's Prize (2006). His novel *Kin* was published in English by Dalkey Archive Press in 2012.

Todd Hasak-Lowy teaches creative writing at the School of the Art Institute of Chicago. His first collection of short stories, *The Task of This Translator*, was published in 2005. His debut novel, *Captives*, appeared in 2008. His translation of Asaf Schurr's novel *Motti* was shortlisted for the Sami Rohr Prize for Jewish Literature.

Hebrew Literature Series

The Hebrew Literature Series at Dalkey Archive Press makes available major works of Hebrew-language literature in English translation. Featuring exceptional authors at the forefront of Hebrew letters, the series aims to introduce the rich intellectual and aesthetic diversity of contemporary Hebrew writing and culture to English-language readers.

This series is published in collaboration with the Institute for the Translation of Hebrew Literature, at www.ithl.org.il. Thanks are also due to the Office of Cultural Affairs at the Consulate General of Israel, NY, for their support.

SELECTED DALKEY ARCHIVE TITLES

Michal Ajvaz, *The Golden Age.*
The Other City.
Pierre Albert-Birot, *Grabinoulor.*
Yuz Aleshkovsky, *Kangaroo.*
Felipe Alfau, *Chromos.*
Locos.
Ivan Ângelo, *The Celebration.*
The Tower of Glass.
António Lobo Antunes, *Knowledge of Hell.*
The Splendor of Portugal.
Alain Arias-Misson, *Theatre of Incest.*
John Ashbery and James Schuyler, *A Nest of Ninnies.*
Robert Ashley, *Perfect Lives.*
Gabriela Avigur-Rotem, *Heatwave and Crazy Birds.*
Djuna Barnes, *Ladies Almanack.*
Ryder.
John Barth, *LETTERS.*
Sabbatical.
Donald Barthelme, *The King.*
Paradise.
Svetislav Basara, *Chinese Letter.*
Miquel Bauçà, *The Siege in the Room.*
René Belletto, *Dying.*
Marek Bieńczyk, *Transparency.*
Andrei Bitov, *Pushkin House.*
Andrej Blatnik, *You Do Understand.*
Louis Paul Boon, *Chapel Road.*
My Little War.
Summer in Termuren.
Roger Boylan, *Killoyle.*
Ignácio de Loyola Brandão, *Anonymous Celebrity.*
Zero.
Bonnie Bremser, *Troia: Mexican Memoirs.*
Christine Brooke-Rose, *Amalgamemnon.*
Brigid Brophy, *In Transit.*
Gerald L. Bruns, *Modern Poetry and the Idea of Language.*
Gabrielle Burton, *Heartbreak Hotel.*
Michel Butor, *Degrees.*
Mobile.
G. Cabrera Infante, *Infante's Inferno.*
Three Trapped Tigers.
Julieta Campos, *The Fear of Losing Eurydice.*
Anne Carson, *Eros the Bittersweet.*
Orly Castel-Bloom, *Dolly City.*
Louis-Ferdinand Céline, *Castle to Castle.*
Conversations with Professor Y.
London Bridge.
Normance.
North.
Rigadoon.
Marie Chaix, *The Laurels of Lake Constance.*
Hugo Charteris, *The Tide Is Right.*
Eric Chevillard, *Demolishing Nisard.*
Marc Cholodenko, *Mordechai Schamz.*
Joshua Cohen, *Witz.*
Emily Holmes Coleman, *The Shutter of Snow.*
Robert Coover, *A Night at the Movies.*
Stanley Crawford, *Log of the S.S. The Mrs Unguentine.*
Some Instructions to My Wife.
René Crevel, *Putting My Foot in It.*
Ralph Cusack, *Cadenza.*
Nicholas Delbanco, *The Count of Concord.*
Sherbrookes.
Nigel Dennis, *Cards of Identity.*
Peter Dimock, *A Short Rhetoric for Leaving the Family.*
Ariel Dorfman, *Konfidenz.*
Coleman Dowell, *Island People.*
Too Much Flesh and Jabez.
Arkadii Dragomoshchenko, *Dust.*
Rikki Ducornet, *The Complete Butcher's Tales.*
The Fountains of Neptune.
The Jade Cabinet.
Phosphor in Dreamland.
William Eastlake, *The Bamboo Bed.*
Castle Keep.
Lyric of the Circle Heart.
Jean Echenoz, *Chopin's Move.*
Stanley Elkin, *A Bad Man.*
Criers and Kibitzers, Kibitzers and Criers.
The Dick Gibson Show.
The Franchiser.
The Living End.
Mrs. Ted Bliss.
François Emmanuel, *Invitation to a Voyage.*
Salvador Espriu, *Ariadne in the Grotesque Labyrinth.*
Leslie A. Fiedler, *Love and Death in the American Novel.*
Juan Filloy, *Op Oloop.*
Andy Fitch, *Pop Poetics.*
Gustave Flaubert, *Bouvard and Pécuchet.*
Kass Fleisher, *Talking out of School.*
Ford Madox Ford, *The March of Literature.*
Jon Fosse, *Aliss at the Fire.*
Melancholy.
Max Frisch, *I'm Not Stiller.*
Man in the Holocene.
Carlos Fuentes, *Christopher Unborn.*
Distant Relations.
Terra Nostra.
Where the Air Is Clear.
Takehiko Fukunaga, *Flowers of Grass.*
William Gaddis, *J R.*
The Recognitions.

Janice Galloway, *Foreign Parts.*
The Trick Is to Keep Breathing.
William H. Gass, *Cartesian Sonata and Other Novellas.*
Finding a Form.
A Temple of Texts.
The Tunnel.
Willie Masters' Lonesome Wife.
Gérard Gavarry, *Hoppla! 1 2 3.*
Etienne Gilson,
The Arts of the Beautiful.
Forms and Substances in the Arts.
C. S. Giscombe, *Giscome Road.*
Here.
Douglas Glover, *Bad News of the Heart.*
Witold Gombrowicz,
A Kind of Testament.
Paulo Emílio Sales Gomes, *P's Three Women.*
Georgi Gospodinov, *Natural Novel.*
Juan Goytisolo, *Count Julian.*
Juan the Landless.
Makbara.
Marks of Identity.
Henry Green, *Back.*
Blindness.
Concluding.
Doting.
Nothing.
Jack Green, *Fire the Bastards!*
Jiří Gruša, *The Questionnaire.*
Mela Hartwig, *Am I a Redundant Human Being?*
John Hawkes, *The Passion Artist.*
Whistlejacket.
Elizabeth Heighway, ed., *Contemporary Georgian Fiction.*
Aleksandar Hemon, ed.,
Best European Fiction.
Aidan Higgins, *Balcony of Europe.*
Blind Man's Bluff
Bornholm Night-Ferry.
Flotsam and Jetsam.
Langrishe, Go Down.
Scenes from a Receding Past.
Keizo Hino, *Isle of Dreams.*
Kazushi Hosaka, *Plainsong.*
Aldous Huxley, *Antic Hay.*
Crome Yellow.
Point Counter Point.
Those Barren Leaves.
Time Must Have a Stop.
Naoyuki Ii, *The Shadow of a Blue Cat.*
Gert Jonke, *The Distant Sound.*
Geometric Regional Novel.
Homage to Czerny.
The System of Vienna.
Jacques Jouet, *Mountain R.*
Savage.
Upstaged.
Mieko Kanai, *The Word Book.*
Yoram Kaniuk, *Life on Sandpaper.*
Hugh Kenner, *Flaubert.*
Joyce and Beckett: The Stoic Comedians.
Joyce's Voices.
Danilo Kiš, *The Attic.*
Garden, Ashes.
The Lute and the Scars
Psalm 44.
A Tomb for Boris Davidovich.
Anita Konkka, *A Fool's Paradise.*
George Konrád, *The City Builder.*
Tadeusz Konwicki, *A Minor Apocalypse.*
The Polish Complex.
Menis Koumandareas, *Koula.*
Elaine Kraf, *The Princess of 72nd Street.*
Jim Krusoe, *Iceland.*
Ayşe Kulin, *Farewell: A Mansion in Occupied Istanbul.*
Emilio Lascano Tegui, *On Elegance While Sleeping.*
Eric Laurrent, *Do Not Touch.*
Violette Leduc, *La Bâtarde.*
Edouard Levé, *Autoportrait.*
Suicide.
Mario Levi, *Istanbul Was a Fairy Tale.*
Deborah Levy, *Billy and Girl.*
José Lezama Lima, *Paradiso.*
Rosa Liksom, *Dark Paradise.*
Osman Lins, *Avalovara.*
The Queen of the Prisons of Greece.
Alf Mac Lochlainn,
The Corpus in the Library.
Out of Focus.
Ron Loewinsohn, *Magnetic Field(s).*
Mina Loy, *Stories and Essays of Mina Loy.*
D. Keith Mano, *Take Five.*
Micheline Aharonian Marcom,
The Mirror in the Well.
Ben Marcus,
The Age of Wire and String.
Wallace Markfield,
Teitlebaum's Window.
To an Early Grave.
David Markson, *Reader's Block.*
Wittgenstein's Mistress.
Carole Maso, *AVA.*
Ladislav Matejka and Krystyna Pomorska, eds.,
Readings in Russian Poetics: Formalist and Structuralist Views.
Harry Mathews, *Cigarettes.*
The Conversions.
The Human Country: New and Collected Stories.
The Journalist.
My Life in CIA.
Singular Pleasures.
The Sinking of the Odradek Stadium.
Tlooth.

SELECTED DALKEY ARCHIVE TITLES

Joseph McElroy,
Night Soul and Other Stories.
Abdelwahab Meddeb, *Talismano.*
Gerhard Meier, *Isle of the Dead.*
Herman Melville, *The Confidence-Man.*
Amanda Michalopoulou, *I'd Like.*
Steven Millhauser, *The Barnum Museum.*
In the Penny Arcade.
Ralph J. Mills, Jr., *Essays on Poetry.*
Momus, *The Book of Jokes.*
Christine Montalbetti, *The Origin of Man.*
Western.
Olive Moore, *Spleen.*
Nicholas Mosley, *Accident.*
Assassins.
Catastrophe Practice.
Experience and Religion.
A Garden of Trees.
Hopeful Monsters.
Imago Bird.
Impossible Object.
Inventing God.
Judith.
Look at the Dark.
Natalie Natalia.
Serpent.
Time at War.
Warren Motte,
Fables of the Novel: French Fiction since 1990.
Fiction Now: The French Novel in the 21st Century.
Oulipo: A Primer of Potential Literature.
Gerald Murnane, *Barley Patch.*
Inland.
Yves Navarre, *Our Share of Time.*
Sweet Tooth.
Dorothy Nelson, *In Night's City.*
Tar and Feathers.
Eshkol Nevo, *Homesick.*
Wilfrido D. Nolledo, *But for the Lovers.*
Flann O'Brien, *At Swim-Two-Birds.*
The Best of Myles.
The Dalkey Archive.
The Hard Life.
The Poor Mouth.
The Third Policeman.
Claude Ollier, *The Mise-en-Scène.*
Wert and the Life Without End.
Giovanni Orelli, *Walaschek's Dream.*
Patrik Ouředník, *Europeana.*
The Opportune Moment, 1855.
Boris Pahor, *Necropolis.*
Fernando del Paso, *News from the Empire.*
Palinuro of Mexico.
Robert Pinget, *The Inquisitory.*
Mahu or The Material.
Trio.
Manuel Puig, *Betrayed by Rita Hayworth.*
The Buenos Aires Affair.
Heartbreak Tango.
Raymond Queneau, *The Last Days.*
Odile.
Pierrot Mon Ami.
Saint Glinglin.
Ann Quin, *Berg.*
Passages.
Three.
Tripticks.
Ishmael Reed, *The Free-Lance Pallbearers.*
The Last Days of Louisiana Red.
Ishmael Reed: The Plays.
Juice!
Reckless Eyeballing.
The Terrible Threes.
The Terrible Twos.
Yellow Back Radio Broke-Down.
Jasia Reichardt, *15 Journeys Warsaw to London.*
Noëlle Revaz, *With the Animals.*
João Ubaldo Ribeiro, *House of the Fortunate Buddhas.*
Jean Ricardou, *Place Names.*
Rainer Maria Rilke, *The Notebooks of Malte Laurids Brigge.*
Julián Ríos, *The House of Ulysses.*
Larva: A Midsummer Night's Babel.
Poundemonium.
Procession of Shadows.
Augusto Roa Bastos, *I the Supreme.*
Daniël Robberechts, *Arriving in Avignon.*
Jean Rolin, *The Explosion of the Radiator Hose.*
Olivier Rolin, *Hotel Crystal.*
Alix Cleo Roubaud, *Alix's Journal.*
Jacques Roubaud, *The Form of a City Changes Faster, Alas, Than the Human Heart.*
The Great Fire of London.
Hortense in Exile.
Hortense Is Abducted.
The Loop.
Mathematics:
The Plurality of Worlds of Lewis.
The Princess Hoppy.
Some Thing Black.
Raymond Roussel, *Impressions of Africa.*
Vedrana Rudan, *Night.*
Stig Sæterbakken, *Siamese.*
Self Control.
Lydie Salvayre, *The Company of Ghosts.*
The Lecture.
The Power of Flies.
Luis Rafael Sánchez,
Macho Camacho's Beat.
Severo Sarduy, *Cobra & Maitreya.*
Nathalie Sarraute,
Do You Hear Them?
Martereau.
The Planetarium.

SELECTED DALKEY ARCHIVE TITLES

Arno Schmidt, *Collected Novellas.*
Collected Stories.
Nobodaddy's Children.
Two Novels.
Asaf Schurr, *Motti.*
Gail Scott, *My Paris.*
Damion Searls, *What We Were Doing and Where We Were Going.*
June Akers Seese,
Is This What Other Women Feel Too?
What Waiting Really Means.
Bernard Share, *Inish.*
Transit.
Viktor Shklovsky, *Bowstring.*
Knight's Move.
A Sentimental Journey: Memoirs 1917–1922.
Energy of Delusion: A Book on Plot.
Literature and Cinematography.
Theory of Prose.
Third Factory.
Zoo, or Letters Not about Love.
Pierre Siniac, *The Collaborators.*
Kjersti A. Skomsvold, *The Faster I Walk, the Smaller I Am.*
Josef Škvorecký, *The Engineer of Human Souls.*
Gilbert Sorrentino,
Aberration of Starlight.
Blue Pastoral.
Crystal Vision.
Imaginative Qualities of Actual Things.
Mulligan Stew.
Pack of Lies.
Red the Fiend.
The Sky Changes.
Something Said.
Splendide-Hôtel.
Steelwork.
Under the Shadow.
W. M. Spackman, *The Complete Fiction.*
Andrzej Stasiuk, *Dukla.*
Fado.
Gertrude Stein, *The Making of Americans.*
A Novel of Thank You.
Lars Svendsen, *A Philosophy of Evil.*
Piotr Szewc, *Annihilation.*
Gonçalo M. Tavares, *Jerusalem.*
Joseph Walser's Machine.
Learning to Pray in the Age of Technique.
Lucian Dan Teodorovici,
Our Circus Presents . . .
Nikanor Teratologen, *Assisted Living.*
Stefan Themerson, *Hobson's Island.*
The Mystery of the Sardine.
Tom Harris.
Taeko Tomioka, *Building Waves.*
John Toomey, *Sleepwalker.*
Jean-Philippe Toussaint, *The Bathroom.*
Camera.
Monsieur.
Reticence.
Running Away.
Self-Portrait Abroad.
Television.
The Truth about Marie.
Dumitru Tsepeneag, *Hotel Europa.*
The Necessary Marriage.
Pigeon Post.
Vain Art of the Fugue.
Esther Tusquets, *Stranded.*
Dubravka Ugresic, *Lend Me Your Character.*
Thank You for Not Reading.
Tor Ulven, *Replacement.*
Mati Unt, *Brecht at Night.*
Diary of a Blood Donor.
Things in the Night.
Álvaro Uribe and Olivia Sears, eds.,
Best of Contemporary Mexican Fiction.
Eloy Urroz, *Friction.*
The Obstacles.
Luisa Valenzuela, *Dark Desires and the Others.*
He Who Searches.
Paul Verhaeghen, *Omega Minor.*
Aglaja Veteranyi, *Why the Child Is Cooking in the Polenta.*
Boris Vian, *Heartsnatcher.*
Llorenç Villalonga, *The Dolls' Room.*
Toomas Vint, *An Unending Landscape.*
Ornela Vorpsi, *The Country Where No One Ever Dies.*
Austryn Wainhouse, *Hedyphagetica.*
Curtis White, *America's Magic Mountain.*
The Idea of Home.
Memories of My Father Watching TV.
Requiem.
Diane Williams, *Excitability: Selected Stories.*
Romancer Erector.
Douglas Woolf, *Wall to Wall.*
Ya! & John-Juan.
Jay Wright, *Polynomials and Pollen.*
The Presentable Art of Reading Absence.
Philip Wylie, *Generation of Vipers.*
Marguerite Young, *Angel in the Forest.*
Miss MacIntosh, My Darling.
Reyoung, *Unbabbling.*
Vlado Žabot, *The Succubus.*
Zoran Živković, *Hidden Camera.*
Louis Zukofsky, *Collected Fiction.*
Vitomil Zupan, *Minuet for Guitar.*
Scott Zwiren, *God Head.*